Not Exactly a War Hero

The Extraordinary Adventures
of Alfred Mondou

Raymond and Smoky with me and my jalopy

Not Exactly a War Hero

The Extraordinary Adventures of Alfred Mondou

Ray Verdon

GSPH

GENERAL STORE PUBLISHING HOUSE INC.
499 O'Brien Road, Renfrew, Ontario, Canada K7V 3Z3
Telephone 1.613.599.2064 or 1.800.465.6072

http://www.gsph.com

ISBN 978-1-77123-054-4

Copyright © Ray Verdon 2013

Cover art, design, illustrations: Magdalene Carson

Printed by Image Digital Printing Ltd.
dba The IDP Group, Renfrew, Ontario
Printed and bound in Canada

Cataloguing data available at Library and Archives Canada

To Canada's zombies, dead or alive

We come from our untold tales that wait for their telling.
We come from Canada, this land that is like every land,
filled with the wise, the fearful, the compassionate, the corrupt.

Kerri Sakamoto

Acknowledgements

In addition to my mother, who passed away only days before the completion of this book, I am grateful to all of my family, Brian Doyle, Shelley Tanaka, Daniel Wiener, and the other Dan, as well as GSPH, for their generous assistance.

Prologue

THE OLD BARN still smelled like hay and oats and sweet manure. On my right, along the wall, I saw rusted scythes, harnesses hanging on pegs, horseshoes propped on a side beam. I saw a rotted wooden washing machine and the stable and mangers beyond.

The sun streamed through the cracks in a dust stream that danced across some timber planks. And to my left stood the cutter. Mac's one-horse shay.

It was a smaller, more pitiful skeleton of the sleigh I remembered, but I saw it with a warmth I can't describe. I had been gone from the barn for a thousand years, but now I saw and smelled and sensed as a boy.

Suddenly, a crow appeared out of the shadows. It hopped onto the sleigh seat where I had always sat with Mac. It looked at me and then fluttered sideways to Mac's spot on the bench.

I stood there staring at the huge, black, silvery-wet bird.

I had to sit with the crow.

As I crawled up onto the bench of the cutter, the crow flew away, but not far. It sat on a rafter above me and looked at me with its wise black eyes. I stared back, trying to be patient. Trying to think like Mac.

The crow will know.

After a time, I looked down at the Calèche de Jos. Ledoux brass plate, the skis and the shafts, and the faded leather seat studded onto the aged and weathered wood. I reached down and touched the compartment beneath the seat. I looked up. The crow seemed to lean forward. My hand touched the rough rug blanket. Fifty years later, the blanket was still waiting in the barn for a sleigh ride. Mac would want me to air it out.

I had trouble extricating it. I got to my knees and saw that the blanket was wrapped in a wide black belt with a big square bronze buckle like Santa Claus would wear. I smiled, thinking Mac might have made the belt. The whole package was jammed tight into the compartment. I got a grip on the belt, pulled out the blanket, and saw that it was wrapped around something. I placed the bundle on the seat, unhooked the belt, and opened up the blanket.

And there it was.

Back in the farmhouse, I dropped my cumbersome bundle in the middle of Mac's dining-room table. The ledger was old, worn leather, deep-stuffed, the spine stretched. When I removed the bands, pages slid sideways onto the table.

It smelled of mothballs, and although many of the pages were faded and stained, for the most part, Mac's firm hand was legible. There were not only pages of writing, but an odd assortment of maps, sketches, and newspaper articles.

On the ledger sheets I could see Mac's neat tallying of accounts, but I was more interested in the notepaper between the pages. Hundreds of crinkly, yellowed pages, sections held together with Niagara clips, each with its own carded identifier: *Sketches, Found Fun, Assorted Maps, Newspapers/Magazines, War and Conscription, Ditties, Last Will and Testament, Talking to Myself,* and a clutter of loose single sheets, memoranda, and finally, photos, and an old, worn, soiled, brown leather book.

The litter of a life, hundreds of pieces all inside a ledger, wrapped in a blanket, bound by a belt, stuffed in a sled, and abandoned in a barn for me to find.

The largest sheaf was at the very bottom, with a card that read, "Letters from the Hereafter." I eased off the clip and smoothed the top sheet.

Dear Raymond,
Remember our trip to the zombie grave in the Hereafter
and that week of adventure in August 1947, Raymond?
Remember that?
How could you forget?

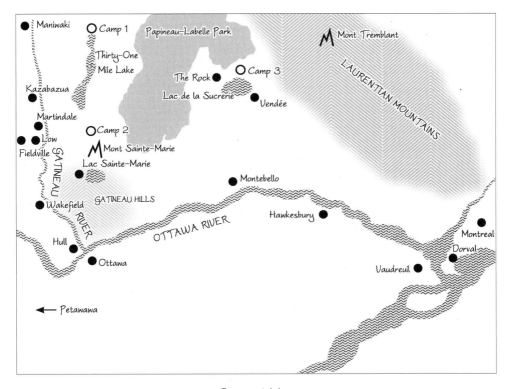

Regional Map
Montreal to Maniwaki

(100 square miles)

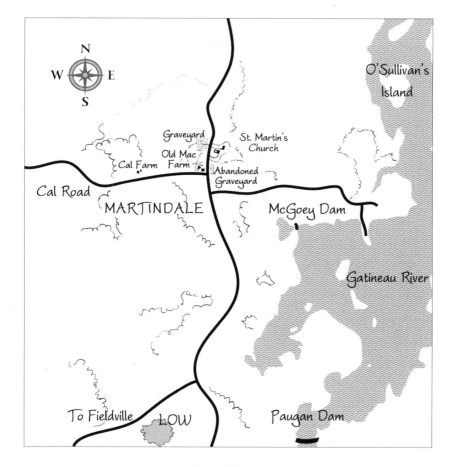

Local Map
Low to O'Sullivan's Island

ONE

August 1947

"JAYSUS!"

Mac lunged from his rocker, tapped the dottle from his pipe, grabbed his .22, and limped full-tilt toward the road.

I started after him, but stopped. I should get Smoky out of the farmhouse, I thought.

Mac turned to me, shook his head and put his finger to his lips in a sh-shing gesture as if he'd read my mind. He circled the blacksmith shop and started up the gravel road toward the graveyard and St. Martin's Church.

I had never seen my uncle move so fast, let alone toward the church. The Hereafter, he called it. He had a perfect view of it and the graveyard from his front porch. Mostly he'd just sit and rock and play his harmonica and stare up at it. "Not a lot of laughter up yon in the Hereafter," he always said.

Something was up.

When Mac neared the top of the hill, he slowed a lot, stepping like he was afraid he'd wake the dead. I did the same. He peered around the thick, bushy sumac and waved me back. Slowly he crept forward until I could see that he was stalking a big, black shadow standing in the graveyard. The shadow was staring down at something. Mac stepped more slowly, stretching to try to see what the shadow was looking at.

Suddenly the shadow turned in our direction. It started moving away, north toward Mac's grove. The dusk was so dull and dark that I could barely see the towering iron cross at the back of the graveyard. The shadow just disappeared into the gloom of the trees. There was no catching it, but Mac didn't seem to care. He just trudged to where the shadow had been standing. He had the straight-ahead look of someone who didn't want to lose his place.

The gravestones were all around us now. Not like the creepy abandoned ones down the hill where I'd go to read the tiny ages on the gravestones. These were all neat and organized in rows—up, down, and across. Mac stared down at one grave-stone, moved to the one to the right of it, and back to his first choice. I was mostly looking at where the shadow had gone. The fog was turning into a cold, misty spray.

"The zombie was looking at this one," Mac muttered.

Mac was talking to himself, which he did all the time, but it was the word "zombie" that did something to my stomach. I knew about zombies from the movies. They were dead folks. Corpses who clawed themselves out of coffins and walked around looking for the brains of dead people to eat.

"Now, that's odd."

What was odd about a grave in a graveyard?

Mac again looked up at the back of the cemetery, nodded, and then got down on one knee and started to read quietly.

"*Alfred Mondou, née 1920* and a dash but there's no date of death. *Je sais qu'il vit.*"

I didn't understand the French stuff, but I noticed the mark at the bottom of the gravestone below the writing. It wasn't a cross like on some of the other gravestones. It was a capital "P" with a "Z" or something scrawled through it.

The misty spray was now turning to rain, clinging to the gravestones and the grass. But Mac just knelt there with his knee in the wet.

I looked around at other gravestones. Egan, O'Malley, Gannon, McCal, McLaughlin. There was a Gleason, like Mac's last name, some French name, and a McCracken, and a McGoey, and a McCay. I was close to figuring out that the small Faye McCay gravestone, not far from where I was standing, was a girl who was nearly nine, just like me. It gave me the heebie-jeebies.

Mac finally stood and turned and, muttering to himself, headed out of the graveyard, and I followed him. The rain was now falling hard and cold on my neck and bare arms. It felt more like early April than August.

That's when I saw Marian standing on the porch of the priest's house beside the church. She was waving at me with her goofy wrist wave. Even through the fog and the rain, I could see her caramel-coloured hair, loose and shining around the brightest, widest smile I had ever seen.

"Besides me, she has the best head in the Gatineau," Mac always said, but he was talking about how smart she was.

I wondered if Marian had seen the Shadow Man, too. I started to wave back at her and then I slipped on the wet grass, slid down to the road, and ripped my elbow on a rock.

I jumped up quickly so she wouldn't think I was a weak little shit. My elbow was bleeding. I rolled down my shirtsleeve to mop up the blood, which was stupid because zombies would be after my brains, not my blood. And if zombies *were* clawing themselves out of coffins, we were dead anyway.

I ran to catch up with Mac to ask him about the strange mark on the gravestone, but he was hunched forward doing his angry grumbling.

"He's like the deer, Raymond," he muttered. "Just appears in the fog. Floats out of the church like a spirit."

I was thinking that Smoky would have caught the zombie if he'd been with us, but instead I said, "Zombies aren't real, Mac."

It was dark now, and as Mac stepped onto his porch, he planted his arm on a pillar, swung around, and put his face right into mine.

"That's what they'd like you to think," he whispered through his gap-toothed grin. "Aaauuuggg-chomp-chomp-chomp."

TWO

January 1942

IT WAS AN OLD CUSTOM in Quebec for an aged farmer to hand over his land to his eldest son, retaining only a life rent. But the real reason Père Mondou conceded the farm to Alfred Mondou's father, Renard, was to get his prodigal son to return to the job at hand. Even as a young teenager, Renard was constantly escaping the confines of the small Fieldville farm to take road and railbed work from Wakefield to Kazabazua.

"You're out there day and night. The cows won't wait. You know that. And I know all about the drinking and *les blondes anglaises*. They're not for you, *tabernac*."

Renard knew it was his responsibility to work the land of *merde* that barely provided enough for a family to live on. After a lifetime on the land, his father was still clearing pine and digging rock and barely eking out an existence on barren soil that was locked in snow and ice for half the year.

So Renard took on the farm and the rest of the family, whose lives centred around the Mondou homestead . . . sisters yet to be married, Mondou cousins, and aunts and uncles with nearby farms.

A small house was built for *Mère* and *Père* only a hundred yards from the farmhouse. Then, on a winter wonderland day, Renard brought his pregnant Colleen home following a ceremony at Holy Name, and a raucous wedding fête was held inside the covered bridge near the village of Fieldville. Colleen quickly gave birth to Marc, Alfred, Céline, Marie, and Claudette. Renard worked the farm, first with his father, and then with sons.

All the while, he was becoming known as one of the finest woodworkers and vivants in the Gatineau. Colleen raised her children and stalked the two solitudes, teaching English or French, whichever was needed.

Renard gave the signed primogeniture paper to his son Marc when he was only fourteen. "It's yours whether you want the fardel or not," he announced.

By 1929, Renard was off to Montebello, often taking his younger son, Alfred, with him. Chateau Montebello was the world's largest log cabin. It was the biggest woodworking job in Quebec's history, and Alfred, without farm, was taught his father's skills. Renard knew that Alfred was more restless than Marc, who was happy to just farm his fields. What Alfred missed in school, Colleen could teach him. The boy was smart, and tall and strong for his age. His "Algonquin soul" showing, his grandmother would always say, but that's another story.

While his father directed men on the massive interior rotunda, Alfred worked with a second, smaller crew on armoires and the additional wings containing the dining room and ball-room. The older men called Alfred "Le P'tit Papineau"—a great compliment, because Louis Joseph Papineau had been the brilliant, cultured, and renowned founder and leader of the seigneury that dominated the area.

P'tit stayed to do cleanup work even after his father left Montebello to grab a longer-term opportunity in Low working at the Paugan Dam. P'tit slept in the chateau stables at night with the other labourers and worked fourteen-hour days until all the finishing touches were complete. By 1932, he was at the Paugan working with his father. Hydro Québec knew that Alfred was underage, but they valued the father-and-son skills so much that they overlooked the issue.

Everyone in the Gatineau began to call the Mondou clan *"le syndicat."* Renard was widely known as *"le patron,"* and he loved it. He could even foresee that Alfred would become the next Mondou *patron*.

"Only God can stop us now, Alfred."

For years, Alfred would wonder if God had considered his father's boast a challenge.

When the Paugan was just about complete, the Gatineau River was diverted into what was known as "the bypass." One day, the man who had been told to open one of the side gates opened the centre one by mistake, just as a log boom was coming down the upper Gatineau. The boom was sucked through the gates by the great force of the current.

A number of men went down with the logs. Some managed to swim ashore, but Renard couldn't swim. Alfred watched with horror as his father was pulverized by a log. They found his battered body two days later. P'tit survived by riding a log down into an eddy of the river and crawling ashore.

At his father's funeral in Fieldville, the Hydro foreman handed P'tit the lumberjack cross made from a rafting pin that his father wore on a clunky chain of linking pins. The gift was a heavy weight that Alfred vowed to never remove. He was fourteen years old.

The young Mondou stayed in Low working at the Paugan, either on the booms, learning the ways of the lumber business, or at the turbines, learning about machinery. By his late teens, he had become skilled at leading men many years older than himself, whether by example or by force. He started to be very well paid by Hydro Québec, and he supported his mother and three sisters, helped his brother on the farm, and managed *le syndicat*, just as his father had predicted.

Then the war came, and no one could foresee God's second strike.

Alfred was served papers to report to Hull to serve in the NRMA, Canada's National Resources Mobilization Act, just after Christmas 1941. Many who hadn't already volunteered were also served. Second sons of local farmers, both Irish and French, workmates on the dam, even a few Algonquins from the Maniwaki reserve.

The NRMA soldiers were conscripted to serve only in direct defence of an enemy assault on Canada, and not for General Service, which made you eligible to be shipped to the Front. Since Mondou and the others assumed that Hitler and his Nazis had higher priorities than an assault on Canada, they felt sure they would never be shipped anywhere to fight anyone. They all gathered in Hull, and they were mad as hell, but they thought the war would be over soon.

The conscripts were shipped from Hull up the river to Camp Petawawa for basic indoctrination. According to Lance Corporal Grafftey, the basics were simple.

"I'm your boss, and there are two kinds of people at Petawawa. A-Men, like that wonderful word that ends a holy prayer. A stands for Active. Men who are willing to serve their God and their country. To go overseas and fight for what they believe in. Courageous and proud men. The other sort, here at the camp, are R-Men. They are not men at all. R stands for Reserves, but I say R stands for Rats. I cannot stomach Reserves. No true Canadian can stomach Reserves, which is why you are called zombies, dead men who are the undead. Chickens, vermin, skunks, weasels, swine. You're not worth a pinch of coon shit. But you can become men. You can become A-Men. Active soldiers. And I will see that you do. Do you understand me?"

What Alfred did not understand was why Grafftey didn't realize that some of the men had no idea what his agitated sermon was all about. They spoke only French. The ones who seemed to understand either stared defiantly at the boss or hung their heads. Alfred would explain the predicament to the others soon enough, and they would all quickly learn together that the differences between A-Men and R-Men went far beyond names.

On the fourth day at Petawawa, P'tit and a dozen others

were ordered out of their barracks in the dead of night by the pudgy lance corporal and four ragged-looking soldiers who always seemed to accompany him. It was brutally cold on the Ottawa River that January night, but the conscripts were not permitted the time to put on overcoats. P'tit was still wearing his rumpled civilian clothes because they had not yet found a uniform big enough for him.

The thirteen conscripts were marched over to a parade ground. They were lined up with their faces against the wall, shivering in the lightly falling snow. Grafftey and the four soldiers stood silently behind them.

After a while, a small detachment marched across the parade ground and stood beside Grafftey, who barked at the conscripts, "Do not turn around. Put your hands up on the wall. You'll know your fate soon enough. And shut up. I want silence."

Alfred placed his hands on the icy wall, and the others then did the same. Grafftey began reading from a document. Alfred understood English well enough, but even he had trouble comprehending the formal declarations in the document. They were being read charges, and their penalty was to be "death by firing squad."

"They do not understand what you are reading," Mondou shouted. "They speak French."

"Bullshit. They will understand this. I'm about to order this squad to be at the ready, and to aim, and to fire. But first we will give you an opportunity. Those of you who show your readiness to serve your country, as millions are doing right now, will be spared. If you want to die here and now, stay where you are. If you want to signal your readiness to serve your country, take three steps backward."

There was a pause, and then another voice shouted, "Soldiers raise your arms."

The raising of the rifles was heard clearly by all the men against the wall.

"READY."

The cocking of the rifles was a sound they all recognized. Mondou, with a look to the side, saw that the others knew what was happening. They were shuddering, and all of them stared back at him, frozen to the wall.

Mondou turned, faced the file of soldiers and shouted, "They don't speak English!"

"Shut up, you coward. Turn around and face the wall."

Alfred stared at Grafftey but did not turn around.

"AIM."

There was a long pause as Alfred just kept staring at the pudgy corporal. With the snow falling more heavily now, he could see it settling gently on the muzzles of the rifles.

How long would they all stand there?

Finally, a soldier from the file turned to Grafftey and said a few words. Without any apparent orders being given, the detachment lowered their arms and marched away into the darkness.

The mock execution was over.

Grafftey ordered the conscripts to stay where they were and marched his four henchmen away. A half hour later, the four men came back without Grafftey, and the thirteen conscripts were led back to their barracks. The largest of the Grafftey gang, a hulk of a man, pointed ominously at Alfred without saying a word as he slowly left the barracks.

Within a week, Mondou and the others knew too well the soldier called Munro, and they all learned everything there was to know about the other differences between an R-Man and an A-Man.

Late one night, almost a month after they arrived, Jacques Dion and Mondou sat on their bunks staring at the red glow of the pot-bellied stove. It was very cold in the barracks, but that was not why they couldn't sleep. Since late evening, Grafftey had been entering and re-entering the barracks with Munro and the rest of his gang of four. They would then disappear with an R-Man who would not return.

It was one more tactic the little lance corporal had been

using since they had arrived at Petawawa. The R-Men would draw more fatigues than A-Men, and endure more inspections that would lead to more browbeating; but Grafftey was saving the best for last.

They came to Jacques.

"Get up and come outside, Dion. We've got papers for you to sign." Grafftey was waving a clipboard, and the same four soldiers were behind him.

Dion stood up and Mondou stood with him, but there was so little room between the bunks that Grafftey found himself staring at Mondou, a tall man with a muscled neck on broad shoulders staring down a broad nose at Grafftey's fat face with puffed slits for eyes.

"Sit down, Mondou. This is not your business."

Mondou just stood and stared at him. Grafftey tilted his head to talk around him to Dion, but Mondou filled too much space, and in the shadows he looked formidable. Now Grafftey's voice rose a couple of octaves, as he looked up and settled on yelling at the ceiling.

"You're a gutless wonder, Dion, and you're playing the rest of us for suckers. Now come outside with us. Commit to serving your flag." Grafftey was now pointing at the ceiling where a large British flag was fastened. It covered the length and width of the barracks.

Neither Mondou nor Dion had to look up. They had stared at the strange flag every night for a month before closing their eyes. On their first night in the barracks Dion had said to Mondou that he couldn't recall ever seeing the flag before.

"We go outside together or we don't go at all," Mondou said to Grafftey.

There was a long silence. Grafftey finally backed away from the bunks and with a flick of his head started out of the barracks with the rest of his entourage trailing behind, except for Munro, who approached Mondou slowly.

In an accent Mondou couldn't recognize he said, "You're

lucky I'm not in charge, you Pepsi frog. You'd be dead right now."

"*Mange la merde*," Alfred said—the one and maybe only French sentence every *anglais* knew.

Munro went red and started toward Mondou.

"Munro!" Grafftey shouted wildly from the door of the barracks. "We need you here."

Munro hesitated and then took another step toward Mondou. "We'll see who will eat shit, you dumb fucking Frenchman."

Mondou and the others slept little that night and learned two things the next morning. First, anyone who hadn't signed the papers was being shipped out of Ottawa Union Station by train to British Columbia the very next day. Second, not one of the men who had suffered through the mock execution had signed up.

As they boarded the train, Grafftey shouted from the platform, "Mondou! We're going to get you and your pussy sisters. You hear me?"

Mondou pretended not to hear. He went to sit in the coach with Jacques. On the platform, Grafftey and Munro were standing only ten yards away, staring at them through the wide train window.

"*Nous sommes les ennemis du peuple*, P'tit," Jacques said quietly.

Mondou was having trouble comprehending how fast his life had changed. He couldn't remember ever having had an enemy. Now, on his twenty-third birthday, he was an enemy of the people. Instead of going northeast forty miles to his home in the Gatineau, he was being shipped a million miles west, to "a pond from which you frogs cannot escape."

Mondou was staggered by the immensity of the country he was seeing. After a full day and night on the train, they still had not left Ontario—Capreol, Hornepayne, Sioux Lookout, Nakina.

The military chaperones were soon paying little attention to their NRMA passengers. The truth of the conscript's choices had been shared generously on day one.

Beyond this train, you could freeze on the sub-zero sweep of a snow-covered lake, huddle to death in the endless bush, or be lucky enough to stumble upon the German POW camp near Capreol. The German guests had learned well the consequences of escape.

Mondou wandered through the two military-assigned rail-cars absorbing fragments of conversation in English and French. He learned that not all of the Quebec conscripts were sent to Terrace, British Columbia. Large groups were being held in buildings on the grounds of the Canadian National Exhibition in Toronto. Others were assigned to units scattered across Canada. Many of the conscripts were not French but came from all parts of the country, and most were not being shipped all the way to Terrace.

He also learned that news of his defiance at Petawawa had spread to everyone. *Encore*, he was *le patron* whether he wanted the role or not.

Early in his walks, he saw a boy, barely seventeen, listening to a group of Quebecers with a look of bewilderment. Mondou introduced himself.

"I'm Keith. Keith Dyck with a 'y,'" the boy said. "They're speaking French, you know."

"You don't speak French?"

"No, I'm from Smiths Falls."

Keith was slight, with a boyish face that was narrow and rather pale. He looked like a child looking for a friend, and too frail to break an egg, let alone fight Germans.

"Well, you're not missing anything. They're saying the same thing you're hearing in English except louder, faster, and angrier."

Mondou was right.

"Volunteer, volunteer, volunteer, a guy at work kept telling me. Then I got called up, and he didn't. Now he's got my job."

"If I could be over there, I would be, but I've got a medical problem."

"What's the problem? No stomach for fighting?"

"It's a cruel way to raise an army. King wants us to make a private declaration of war. Why don't they choose in the Parliament? It turns us against each other. Even families. My pop went to the big one when he was almost forty and never came back. My mom and brother say no."

"You Pepsis are lucky. You get to hide behind Quebec politicians like Duplessis. The whole fucking province is on your side. In the rest of the country, we're lepers."

Mondou did come to understand that it was easier to be a Quebec zombie. The French were a fraternity. The choice for *les anglais* seemed more solitary.

As he wandered the cars, he felt the tension building. He was beginning to wonder whether a country could be too big. There were so few people across the expanse of northern Ontario, Manitoba, Saskatchewan, and Alberta, and so many of the young were going to war. Outside there was endless horizon; inside the train, there were just frayed nerves and threats, one hundred hours of wheels clicking against rails, and endless time for agitators to rework the same diatribes over and over again.

The French fraternity would frequently break into rounds of "Alouette." The officers and General Service men would respond with a song of their own, sung to the tune of "My Darling Clementine":

> So I joined the Active Service,
> Sailing over with the tide,
> I can walk along the street now,
> Never have to go and hide.

Now come listen, all you zombies,
You drink our wine, you drink our beer,
But you won't turn General Service,
For a handcuffed volunteer.

That's the end of our story,
All you zombies, please take heed,
Why not join the Active Service,
Help us out where'er there's need.

The first fight on the train was not French against English, however.

Mondou knew there was something not quite right about the boy, Keith, sitting at the table with the three English. There were cards on the table but they did not seem to be playing as Mondou stopped beside them. Keith was unfolding a paper.

"This is the letter from my brother. He's fighting in Italy." Keith was beaming. "I'll carry this letter everywhere until he sends the next one, and then I store the old one in my pack. I have every one." Keith held the letter like it was an injured bird.

"He says, I know it's tough, Keith. The pressure is on for you guys to Go Active but don't come over here. Stay in Canada, closer to Nancy and Joe and Mom. If they force you to come, okay, but it's not fair for both of us to be here so don't volunteer." Keith looked up and said, "My brother doesn't know I'm being shipped west so I won't be here, or there. I'm going to purgatory."

The bald and burly Jake bellowed as he reached across the table and grabbed the letter from Keith's hand, "Shut up, you little whiner. What'd you do? Write the fucking letter yourself? You play cards with no money. You whine about the war." And he crumpled the letter into a ball.

Keith, with a cry, lunged desperately across the table just as Mondou clutched Jake's forearm. Jake jerked hard, but his arm barely moved. He started to swing his left arm across, but

Mondou clutched the other forearm, then quickly squeezed and twisted Jake's elbows, forcing them back into his stomach.

"Now, just open that hand and drop the letter on the table," Mondou whispered.

"This is none of your fucking business, Frenchy." And Jake spat in Mondou's face.

Mondou hunched his shoulders and twisted more forcefully, until the scream, "Charlie, do something!"

As Charlie rose over the table to take a swing, Mondou released Jake's right arm, drove his fist into Charlie's nose with his left, and instantly grabbed the letter arm again. Now Jake and Charlie were both groaning, with Charlie spitting blood, and the third man trapped by the table sitting quietly.

"Drop the letter, Monsieur Jake, or you will not be able to use these arms for a year." Mondou twisted again, Jake yelped, and the letter dropped from his grasp.

"Pick it up, Keith. Go and have a seat in the back car. I'll be there soon," Mondou said calmly.

Sergeant Dolan and two officers were seated in the last quadrant of seats by the door that led out to the vestibule between the cars, watching everything unfold. When one of the lieutenants rose to stop the fight, Dolan shook his head.

"Let it play out. Lets out some steam."

Mondou lifted and spread Jake's arms so he was splayed like a butchered turkey. Then he moved his big face so close to Jake that they almost touched. He wanted Jake to feel the breath in his words, to make sure this *anglais* was in line. He had to make fear smother the man's anger, or he would never go away.

"I apologize for interrupting your card game, Monsieur Jake, but listen carefully. Fight me, fight my gang. Trouble the boy or me again, and we will all be spitting on your grave. *Comprends*?"

"How strong do you have to be to do that? He played that goof like a puppet. We can use that guy. Now get Doc to fix up that broken nose over there."

THREE

August 1947

THAT NIGHT, Mac and I were playing checkers and listening to "The Bum Song" on the spring-operated Victrola. It was Mac's favourite. The song was by a country singer called Haywire Mac, and Great-aunt Gertie called it Mac's anthem. Mac would sing the chorus, "I'm on the bum again," knowing he would get a laugh because folks thought he was always on the bum.

Mom said it wasn't his fault. Mac was just in the wrong place at the wrong time.

"He was an apprentice to his father the blacksmith, but the Iron Vulcan Works died. He rode the rails west to find work, but it was the Depression. He came back to this poor excuse for a farm but he was no farmer. Your great-uncle is unlucky in work."

"And in love," Gertie would always add. "He should have been a priest. That would have solved both problems." And then both of them would laugh. Sometimes they laughed so hard they cried, but they never said any of this when Mac was around.

Some folks took to calling Mac "Haywire," not only because he loved "The Bum Song" so much, but because they all thought he was crazy.

While Mac stared at the checkerboard, I stared at Mac. He had a face that could scare a kid even if you weren't looking at it through the flickering of a coal-oil lamp. The grotesque goitre on his neck stood out the most. His chin and jawbone were especially broad and held a wide, thin mouth full of rotten teeth. He had a blotchy, bulbous nose drooping over a leathered face, which Mom said made people think Mac was a drinker, but he was probably the only Irishman in Upper Low who was a teetotaler.

His bottom-half always looked shabby. It was because his pants were so big they would have fallen down if it wasn't for suspenders; sort of like clown pants.

Below the brim of his fancy straw hat, his eyes were large, sunken and penetrating. He always hung a big handkerchief from his back pocket and wore his dapper straw hat even when he worked in the fields, which he didn't do much. He called the straw his Sunday go-to-church hat but he never went to church, either, and that's another reason most folks thought he was loony.

Aunt Gertie told me it was a face only a nephew could love.

"You won't find a more remarkable face in the Gatineau," my mom would respond, but I think that was her way of saying the same thing as Gertie.

He had an old car he called his jalopy. He also had a one-horse sleigh in the back barn, but he didn't have a horse to pull it, which upset him because he was always promising to take me on a sleigh ride at Christmas, but that's another story.

I was telling Mac about zombies. About how I loved to go to the movies with the other kids in Ottawa, to the Imperial or the Rat Hole on Bank Street on Saturday afternoon and see a cartoon and a serial and then three movies.

I was telling him about *Revenge of the Zombies.*

"This mad doctor makes living dead zombies for the Nazis, and . . ."

"Raymond," Mac whispered, "forget I mentioned the zombies. Do you want to see the symbol? The one on the gravestone?"

I nodded, even though I had forgotten all about it. I was too busy worrying about zombies. My friend Buster Burns said zombies were a load of crap, just like Santa Claus. He said zombies were just in the movies; but Mac didn't go to the movies, and he wasn't crazy like folks said, and he was talking about zombies like they were real. Mac wouldn't even tell me there was a God when we all knew there was one. Mac said he believed in Cosmo instead. That was his name for everything around us—the trees, the fields, the animals, the rain and storms, the people in China and India, and everything. He'd look up from the back pasture and tell me the stars were Cosmo's toenails, and they'd never find Cosmo's head because he had no beginning and no end, and I laughed and said that's what it said about God in my catechism, but I think he already knew that.

I was sitting there thinking all that and rubbing Smoky, who was sitting beside my chair with his head on my lap.

Mac made his move, gave me his one-minute signal and then got up and hunched over to his tall secretary desk, the one I loved because there seemed to be so many secrets inside. Mom called it his reliquary. Mac kept his books under his bed but there were two books he kept in the secretary. One was an Oxford dictionary and the other was a big red Bible.

This time he pulled out the Bible. I could have guessed it would be the Bible, because when I was visiting and he wanted the dictionary he'd always make me get it and I would have to look up the word and then read the definition to him. He said it was good for me to read the definition because then I'd be more likely to remember it.

As for the Bible, he was always telling us that we should read that as well. The trouble with Catholics, he said, was they let the priests do all the reading, and they just sat and listened to the guy in the pulpit.

"You don't need priests to do your thinking for you."

He put the Bible down beside me and opened it, and in a

page or two, right near the beginning, he stopped and pointed at a symbol.

"That's what they call a monogram, Raymond. This one is a combination of an X and a P. Those are the first two letters of the Greek word for Christ. Chi, which is the X, and P, which is Rho. 'ChiRho,' or Christ. This symbol was used by early Christians, but you'll still see it around a bit, often in graveyards."

"But Mac, the sign the zombie was looking at wasn't like this one—"

"Raymond, let's test your arithmetic. Remember the gravestone? How old would Mondou be if he was still alive?"

Well, I hated arithmetic so I pretended to ignore him and focus on my move. Mac just sank his head low over the checker table, looking into my eyes.

"Raymond, how old would Mondou be?"

"Who's Mondou?"

I knew it was the name on the gravestone, and he knew I knew.

"He was born in 1920, and it's now 1947. How old would he be now?"

Mac wasn't about to say another word until I answered, so after a while I blurted it out.

"Twenty-seven and gone to heaven," he chuckled over and over, while he made sucking sounds on his pipe.

Mac was always chuckling to himself. Mom said he'd learned to amuse himself through the long and lonely winters. If you listened carefully, you could usually find out what he was cackling about because a ditty would pop out eventually. "Give me time and I'll find the rhyme," he'd say, or he'd sing about the daughter of someone named O'Malley:

Mr. O'Malley where's your daughter,
We've come down to have some fun.
She's gone out to make her water
She'll be in as soon as she's done.

"Between the old Gatineau ones and my made-up ones, I'll bet I have damned near a hundred ditties," Mac would say, and then he'd sing another.

My mother moved toward us from the table that sat in front of the big black stove.

"What is so interesting about that grave up there?"

Mac was ready for her. He'd often talk about how the women could hear everything we said no matter where they were. He'd say that the only times he was ever wrong was when Gertie was listening.

"That grave has an interesting inscription," Mac said.

My mother waited.

"It's in French and it reads, 'I know that he lives,'" he finally said.

"Yep," said my mother, "and so do lots of graves. That's what it says on Handel's grave in London." She winked at me.

"That's not exactly right, Rita. That's not what it says on Handel's grave." And then Mac chanted, "Twenty-seven and gone to heaven," over and over.

"What are you babbling about, Old Mac?" Gertie said.

"Just thinkin' I'd tell foolish Father Foley he has a zombie in his graveyard."

"Shut your yap. And don't be telling Raymond about the zombies. And don't call the good Father foolish."

Aunt Gertie always said Mac hated priests so much because his fiancée ran away with one just before Mac went west to find work during the Depression.

Mac didn't say another word about zombies until I went up to bed.

"When the girls are gone to the city," he whispered, "we're going to find ourselves a zombie."

Now I knew for sure that Buster Burns was wrong. If Gertie didn't want me to know about them, and Mac was going to look for them, they were out there, all right.

That night I lay in bed with Smoky, listening to the sounds.

It was amazing how many sounds there were. A summer night was not a quiet night. There were crickets, the train whistle heading south to Ottawa. I could hear the bats' wings and their squeaks. Some nights they seemed to explode into the sky above the porch roof, and other times they seemed to come in a row, like they were taking turns. Mac said it depended on what the bugs were doing. He'd built houses for the bats on the sides of his outbuildings simply by nailing old planks onto the wall.

"It's why we don't have bugs," he'd say.

When I heard their swoosh, I peeked up over the windowsill and watched them by the pale light from the windows. I was also looking up at the graveyard for signs of zombies.

I heard Proulx's loud French accent on his way in from the road. Proulx always talked loud even if he was sitting right beside you. He must have thought everyone was deaf.

"Shouldn't raise bats, Old Mac. They cause consumption, you know."

Proulx was a French Canadian who lived on his farm down by the river. I guess he was as lonely as Mac. He usually walked up when Mac was alone; or waited until he thought I was in bed, and then he and Mac would argue well into the night.

I had a secret listening post underneath the front parlour window behind Mac's big secretary, where I could curl up and hear everything the grown-ups said as they rocked and talked on the front porch. Usually Aunt Gertie and my mom went out to join Mac with their tea, but they were going back to Ottawa the next morning so they had turned in early. I heard them and their mattresses moan as they crawled into bed.

I closed Smoky in the bedroom and snuck down to my post.

By the time I got there, Mac was already into one of his tales.

"It was around eleven o'clock and I was rocking here on the porch, and a long, black car pulled up and parked near the blacksmith shop. Mackenzie King got out of the back of the car and walked right over just like you would, Proulx. Asked me to call him Rex. Said he'd heard in Kingsmere that the Martindale ghosts are restless, and that they talk to each other from the lower graveyard to the upper graveyard.

"'Yep,' I told him. 'Right there by the shop, the veil between our world and the spirit world is the thinnest, Rex.'

"He asked for an upright chair from inside the house and went out to the road and spoke to the driver, who pulled out and went up the hill. Then Rex sat in the darkness against the shop wall between the two graveyards.

"Driver came back down the hill exactly an hour later. Must have been sitting in the church lot looking down at his boss. Then Rex brought the chair back to me.

"'Mac,' he said, 'Isabel was there. I heard her voice. She said, 'You did well, Willie. But your job is done. I'm looking forward to seeing you soon.'

"He reached down to shake my hand and said, 'I'll be back, Mac.' Then he walked to the car and drove away, and hasn't come back yet."

"Are you talking about our prime minister, Mac?"

"How many Mackenzie Kings do you know?"

I knew Proulx would spread that one around faster than he spread manure.

After that, they went back to the same old arguing. They argued about only two things—religion and Mac's laziness—and as I settled into my listening post, they were at it again. Proulx was very religious. He was always trying to talk Mac into going up to Mass.

"You'll not earn your way into heaven by doin' the priest's dirty work and draggin' me up the hill, Proulx. You work like a jerk and pray away the rest of the day. You're boring me, so give yourself a rest."

"Mac, you must learn the power of the confessional. No matter how deeply you offend God, he will forgive you. Even murder, Mac."

"That must be handy for you, Proulx. How many murders

are you up to now? I thought I'd be at the top of your list but I'm still kickin'."

"Murder is not funny, Mac. It's a mortal sin. I know you don't like your Père Foley, so come up to the French Mass with Père Beaubien. He could hear your confession in English, and—"

Mac exploded. "Foley may be full of shit, Proulx, and walking around all the time with his head in his breviary so he don't have to talk to folks, but your Père thinks his shit don't stink, and he's guilty of the sin of pride, which is the worst of all sins. After you get him down here on his knees asking for my forgiveness I'll consider goin' up the hill. Now shut your gob and stop using me to try and save your own soul."

But Proulx never shut his gob. "You're a pagan, Mac. And you'll spend eternity in the fires of hell."

"If they don't let your fool priests marry and be normal, your whole goddamned church is going to hell, Proulx. The way Foley and Beaubien get along, it's queer. Maybe your priests are queer."

I thought Proulx would leave after that, because he had a real bad temper, but he didn't this time. I knew other folks also wondered about how well the two priests got along. Usually French priests and English priests never had anything to do with each other, and they even reported to different bishops. Foley couldn't speak a word of French, yet the two priests would cover for each other at Mass. Mac just laughed, "It's in Latin, so no one knows what's going on."

Once Proulx felt that he wouldn't be able to talk Mac into going to Mass, he started trying to talk him into going to work. Proulx never lost his train of thought with Mac. It was churching or farming—the two things he knew Mac hated most.

"Guilty of the deadly sin of sloth, you are, Mac," he said. "This would be a better farm if you did even a lick of work."

"I'm a lily of the field, Proulx. I will not sow or reap or toil, and I sure as hell won't stook. You ever notice that the Bible says God worked six days to create the universe, and rested for eternity? He's lazier than me. Adam and Eve could have loafed forever in Eden if the serpent hadn't done them in. Even Jesus got tired of being a carpenter. Then he goes and talks the disciples out of being fishermen, or tax collectors, and they all just wander around shooting the breeze. If he'd worked in some jokes, I would have been a disciple."

I had to cover my mouth to choke back the laughter. I was sure Proulx was crossing himself over and over to keep Mac's evil away.

Mac said that back in Greek and Roman times and through the Middle Ages, work was considered vulgar, and physical labour was only for slaves and serfs.

"Then came the damned Calvinists with their work ethic. Jesus would have made a piss-poor Calvinist, don't you think? It's a good thing he was a Catholic, I'm thinking. Good thing he came back from the dead." He laughed real hard at that, and then he suddenly got serious. "Just like that French zombie of yours, eh, Proulx? Whatever happened to him, anyway?"

"He got killed by the army."

"Some believe he lives, Proulx. And what about the other one? The American?"

"I don't want to talk about him, either. He rented my barn. Marie said we needed the money. Besides, you said America don't have zombies."

"Yep, I told you that because he was a draft dodger. He couldn't go back to America. They shoot draft dodgers. But where did he go?"

"*Maudit, tabernac*, I told you before. I made him go away when you said the Americans would shoot him. I didn't want no trouble."

"Where did he go?"

"How do I know? Quebec is a big country. Montreal, maybe."

"Where is the French zombie?"

"I told you. I don't talk about the French zombie. Why do you care so much about zombies? *Tabernac*, I'm tired of all these secret things with you."

I heard the top of the rocker slam against the wall as Proulx jumped up.

"*Bon soir*, Old Mac. You're crazy like they all say."

I slipped away from my post and ran up the stairs before Mac came in for the night. I got into bed with Smoky and wondered why Proulx was so mad. Mac said Proulx's French swear words were all about religious stuff in the church, so he only swore when he was very, very angry.

It seemed like zombies were making Proulx angry, and Mac curious.

It's too bad Buster Burns was wrong about zombies. Because now I knew for double sure they were real and I sure didn't want to help Mac find them.

FOUR

November 1944

BY 1944, TERRACE, British Columbia, was the home of the 15th Infantry Brigade, made up of the PEI Highlanders, the PA Volunteers from Saskatoon, the 19th Field Ambulance Corps, and the Fusiliers du Saint-Laurent. Mondou became a fusilier thanks to years of target practice in the back bush as a boy.

At Terrace there was not the level of intimidation he had endured with Grafftey and Munro at Petawawa. Nonetheless, the Reserves were constantly reminded that army strategy had not changed. The words of Canada's commanding officers were etched on the minds of each and every one of them: "We'll make it as tough as possible on you bastards until you decide to go Active."

Over time, the strategy worked. By 1944, more than 58,000 of the NRMA had been helped to see the error of their ways. The rest, who stayed as Reserves, were at their wits' end.

The 15th at Terrace consisted mostly of NRMA troops strongly opposed to being conscripted. About 40 percent of them were from Quebec, yet Quebec continued to be the second-largest provincial source for every General Service branch of the military.

As for the draftees at Terrace, there was no possible way to desert from the northeast interior of British Columbia, so they simply served their time while becoming more and more anxious about their "R" status.

Except for Mondou.

He was tired of the bullying from the army, but just as weary with the bitching from his friends. "*La situation*" was discussed interminably. He was so tired of it all. The only interminable problem for Mondou was his family in Fieldville. He worried about his mother, his brother Marc, now with wife and child, and his sisters still unmarried. They could not survive well with only the farm. Occasionally, he heard from more recent recruits from the Gatineau that his Fieldville tribe was in trouble. Marc was drinking too much, and the Mondou relatives were having crises of their own.

He wept at his helplessness. The pain of absence from a family that needed him was mixed with an unaccustomed fear. He had not been able to save his *père* at the dam. Now, except for sending home much of his meagre pay, he had not been able to help his family for three years, and there seemed to be no end to it.

Mondou had even considered going Active, since he was not available to his family anyway, but that decision became more complicated. For fear of voter reaction, politicians continued to refuse to cast a vote in Parliament forcing the conscripts to go overseas to the fighting fields. It was so much easier to let the army draft who they wanted, as Reserves if necessary, and then intimidate them into volunteering without the issue ever coming to a vote.

But by late 1944, so many Allied soldiers were dead or maimed that regiments were now going into battle several hundred men short of full strength. Mondou knew the remaining conscripts were the obvious answer. Active service must be enforced on everyone, and he fully expected Parliament to recognize that soon. He started to talk openly about going Active.

He expected abuse from his friends, but not resistance from the army. A senior officer had decided that he wanted Mondou to avoid General Service and stay at Terrace. The commander at

Terrace had come to agree.

As was his way, Mondou had focused on work to escape everything else. It was the only way he could stop himself from going insane. He had a very low tolerance for boredom. Unlike his friends who were just going through the motions, Alfred had become one of the rare Reserves who devoted himself to his assignments. In addition to regular training and marksmanship and hand-to-hand combat, he was working on special projects in the motor pool.

His old friends were not impressed.

"Jacques, can you not stop talking about this?" Mondou said. "All of you will go crazy before you go Active if you don't get busy with something else, or just make a goddamned choice. The prime minister has promised a hundred times in front of Parliament and everyone in Canada. We will not be sent overseas. So you volunteer or you don't volunteer. No need to talk morning, noon and night, month after—"

"Fuck you, Mondou."

"Your English is improving, Jacques."

"Fuck you, Mondou. Mackenzie King is full of shit and so are you. King will change his mind any day now. He is a politician. He'll not stand by his word through all of this. And you? What decision have you made? You play with your army toys morning, noon, and night. You talk about going Active but you wait like the rest of us. Fuck you."

"*Touché, mon vieux*. You're right, and about King, too."

"It's getting ugly, Alfred. We have to protect our status. The government cannot be allowed to change its mind. You're ignoring all of it, but you won't be allowed to ignore it when it happens here. You'll have to choose sides."

Mondou had heard all the same stories lately. NRMA groups and their supporters were protest marching with loaded arms and burning flags across Canada.

"I can smell it on you, Mondou. You've changed sides," Onesime once shouted at him.

Alfred's complication with the army was also coming to a peak. Everyone knew he was the subject of a serious tug-of-war between two of the most senior officers at Terrace.

On the one hand, Mondou could handle a rifle, was a superb sharpshooter, and, being exceptionally strong, he had become an expert at hand-to-hand combat.

Sergeant Dolan, in charge of base training, said, "We teach everyone the same way, but this son of a bitch is as strong as steel, learns instantly, and has guts enough to make the strike. The man is a warrior, and I'll get him into combat. He'll be a good example."

On the other hand, Sergeant Williams, in charge of armament engineering and the motor pool, quickly discovered that Mondou had skills that he did not have access to elsewhere in Canada's army. He did not want Mondou transferred anywhere, including the Front, until their job was done.

Mondou could build or fix anything. He was given special status and put to work on the early development of Tracked Vehicles. Before Mondou arrived, Tracked Vehicles was only a great project on paper. It was a job made in heaven as far as Alfred was concerned. It took his mind off "*la situation*."

The army wanted a caisson-like armoured vehicle that could move rapidly over any terrain in any season. Different ideas were merging. It started as a half-track vehicle with tank treads on the back and rubber wheels on the front. It looked like a pickup truck dragging a broken axle at its rear end. But it was far too slow.

For winter conditions, Mondou had the answer. They thought he was a genius, but he had already seen what was needed at the Paugan only a few years earlier. He proved to everyone that rugged skis reinforced with wear bars and a tank tread driving belt would deliver far more speed and versatility riding over snow and frozen ground. It was something no one at Terrace had ever imagined. The prototype had to be engineered, but they soon knew it was the winter solution.

The question remained: "What about the rest of the year?"

On a field trip through the Kootenays with the ski tank, Mondou and Williams came across a Japanese internment camp. Twenty-two thousand Japanese–Canadian citizens were interned in the Kootenays during the war for fear they were enemies of the people. At one of the camps, Mondou and Williams watched a vehicle race through the bush toward them on enormous tire wheels. They befriended the two old Japanese captives who had built their own machine using tractor tires. All-terrain vehicles had been in use in mountainous areas of Japan for years. They finally bought the machine from the Japanese and launched Project JAP. Sergeant Williams told everyone it was an acronym for Job Assignment Protocol. He and Mondou laughed at the reports they were filing in Ottawa under the name.

After four more months in the motor pool, Mondou was given control of JAP. He focused on the two separate vehicles. One for winter snow with skis, and the alternate for the rest of the year with truck tires. They had to increase the size and power of both machines for effective use by the military. Mondou was given the resources, and one year later, Mondou, Sergeant Williams, and an engineer had seized the opportunity of chinook-like weather for a November trial run down the Kitimat with their JAP tire tank.

The chinook run, which was to be three days and two nights, lasted almost a week because of unusual rains that caused slides and washouts.

It turned out to be an eventful week back at the camp.

By mid-November 1944, King's government faced disaster over the lack of reinforcements for the army overseas. It had become a national disgrace and was becoming an international one. King's ministers were threatening to resign. To save himself, King had to give in. Parliament was called, and they approved shipping zombies abroad immediately. Jacques's prediction had finally come true.

The prime minister's announcement triggered the Terrace mutiny, which lasted from November 23 to November 29. It became the most serious breach of military discipline in Canadian history. It started simply as an anti-conscription parade of 1,500 NRMA members and evolved into a rebellion of close to a thousand soldiers armed with Stens. Eventually, they commandeered a drill hall and armoury while the brigade's senior officers were away from Terrace at a meeting. The mutineers kidnapped two junior officers and broadcast their intention not to be shipped overseas. Dozens were inside the armoury with their captives while hundreds circled outside showing their support. The mutineers expected that the deceit shown by Mackenzie King would be exposed and publicized in all of Canada's media, and a movement would begin to reverse the decision of Parliament.

When Mondou returned from the Kitimat run on November 25th, his friends from Petawawa had been inside the armoury for a day and a half. The mutineers who had been circling outside had disappeared or been gathered up and confined with the help of reinforcements from Prince Rupert.

Mondou sat on the edge of his cot staring out the barracks window toward the armoury. He heard footsteps behind him. He turned to watch Sergeant Williams approach and then stand at the foot of his bed. They both stared out the window.

"I told them there was no need to put you in lock-up, Alfred. You're lucky to be out here. Your friends won't be safe long if they insist on holding the armoury. If they hurt one of the captives or even fire a shot, they'll wish they'd gone to the Front. Reinforcements and weapons are in the marshalling area over there." Williams nodded toward the parade square not more than a hundred yards away. "A lot of those soldiers are tired of training. They would just love to shoot at someone, and no one is going to try hard to stop them. Most of them hate zombies more than Nazis anyway."

Mondou nodded.

Williams watched the armoury for another few moments and finally said, "Get some sleep, Alfred. We've had a long week, and we're about to consign two great products. Don't let me down. Goodnight."

Mondou sat alone in the fading light emptying his mind to the task ahead. It was simple, really. He'd run hard and be shot, maybe by a comrade, or he would make it to the armoury, where he'd convince Jacques and the others to come to their senses.

What was the alternative? Just wait helplessly to witness a tragedy? His friends were inside that armoury.

At 11:15, he decided. "*Bien,* into the breach."

Mondou made it to the armoury. There were shouts to stop, but he heard only one shot, and a thud from behind as he rounded the armoury. He worked his way along the right side of the building until he found the door and identified himself through the slot. He was greeted heartily and welcomed to the mission.

The attitude toward him changed quickly once he began to argue one-on-one and in groups. He spent half the night and most of the following day making his case for surrender. Others argued just as aggressively that they had control of the armoury and should fight back. Jacques and some of his closest friends avoided him.

Mondou's lobbying finally led to an assembly late the following afternoon, long after he thought the reinforcements would already have attacked. He guessed they were waiting for the cover of darkness.

Mondou climbed onto the long counter that ran in front of the racks of guns and ammunition in the marshalling area.

"We've got guns but they've got bigger guns and they know how to use them," he said. "You won't go and shoot Germans but you'll shoot Canadians. You think that will help your cause?"

"Do they know about us?" someone shouted back. "Has it been on the radio? Do they know why we're doing this?"

"I don't think so. I've been down the Kitimat but there was

no sign of any press around here when we pulled back in yesterday afternoon. Look out there. There's nothing but soldiers and officers who hate us more than ever. They want to shoot Nazis, but we'll be good practice."

"No one will shoot at us as long as we have them." Someone pointed at the two captives, who were sitting unbound, watching the events as if they were at a local hockey game.

"What kind of press will you get if you hurt them?" Mondou said.

The arguments went around and around, and dark was falling.

"Where are the others who were helping us outside?"

"They've been imprisoned in the lock-up, or in their barracks. They're finished."

Onesime mounted the other end of the counter and waited until he had everyone's attention. Then he looked at Mondou.

"And why aren't you in the lock-up, Monsieur Mondou? Why are you not arrested?"

Onesime paused and, as if on cue, someone shouted, "Because he's one of them. He's their fucking spy. He's a *maudit* fucking *anglais*."

"You're a traitor to your people, you goddamned fucking bastard!" Onesime yelled as he launched himself into a run down the counter, and with one lunge they both collapsed into the racks of equipment.

The sound of the blasts came at exactly that moment. For one long minute, Mondou thought they were all dying. The blasts were so loud that the zombies were deafened, and the armoury trembled. There was heat, a burning smell, a long-lasting incandescent light, and a metallic taste in every mouth.

It was only one long convulsion but it was enough. They were scared shitless.

Thanks to Mondou, Onesime remained unconscious through it all. He was out cold when Mondou regained control of the mutineers and arranged the surrender.

FIVE

August 1947

MOM LEFT FOR OTTAWA on Friday morning because Gertie had to get back to work taking care of an old lady. I think Gertie was older than the old lady but she was a tough one.

I had an extra week before school started. Mom wanted me to go home with her, but I never went back to the city before I had to.

I wasn't sure I wanted to hunt for a zombie, and I had told the Cals that I'd be in to do some milking and stooking after my mom went home. So as soon as they left, and Mac hunched out to the shop, I brought Smoky into the farmhouse and filled his bowl and hightailed it to Cals'.

The Cals were my cousins sort of second-removed, Mom said. There was Aunt Mabel and Uncle Martin and their kids, Billy and Brian and Betsy, and about forty milking cows, and sometimes a bull and calves, and lots of pigs and chickens, and dogs who worked rounding up the cows, and pups that just hung around with cats that licked up the spillings from the dairy. The Cals were busy and got so used to my coming back and forth in the summers, I didn't know whether they knew I was there or not half the time.

I could walk across fields or along the road, because the two farms were neighbours, and it was less than two miles. I could stay overnight with my cousins in Billy and Brian's room, but I usually didn't want to when there was too much work to be done.

"You're just like Old Mac. Work appears, you disappear," Billy said, but nobody could outwork those two. Brian was my age, and Billy a few years older, and they worked harder than anyone I ever knew in the city—even fathers with jobs.

After one day at Cals' I still wasn't sure that I wanted to go zombie hunting, but I also knew that it wasn't raining; so after milking, there'd be another day of stooking in the fields in the hot sun. Nothing was worse than piling up bales of oats and leaning them in a teepee so they'd dry in the sun. You either had too much clothing and the heat would get you, or too little and the nettles and thistles would scrape you, and you'd itch for a week. You had to wear gloves because the twine would tear up and blister your hands. After a long while, when you'd finished a small corner of the field, you'd look up and see bales staggered across the sea of stubble as far as the horizon. They were waiting like leeches.

So after milking on Saturday, I snuck away from Cals', walked back by the road, and cut the Martindale corner by crossing the back field toward Mac's house. I was hungry because Cals ate breakfast after milking, but I didn't want to stick around for that because then they'd have me organized and stooking for another day.

Suddenly, I saw Smoky bounding through the oats at full speed with his red bandana bouncing above and below the oats like a robin bobbing low.

Smoky was as black as coal with a white triangle on his throat. Aunt Gertie said he got his name because he was black, but Mac said if you looked it up, smoky meant a charcoal-grey colour.

"Nope," he said. "Smoky got his name because of how he smelled. When we're in at night, and the old stove's going full, and folks are smoking their cigarettes, and me on my pipe, you just take Smoky outside for a minute. He smells like a stinking ashtray. That's why your mom and I called him Smoky."

He always wore a red bandana. Mom and I had three so one would always be clean.

"Oh, but he is a handsome dog," Mac liked to say. "You can tell by the way he romps that he knows it."

Smoky lived in Ottawa with me, except for the summer, when he stayed with Mac because I was up the Gatineau all the time anyway. Smoky was a border collie-Labrador mix. He could herd things, and chase things, and sing and dance to Mac's harmonica.

Smoky reached me and leaped and licked and moaned and groaned until I'd had enough of rolling around in the oats. Then he stared at me with his bright eyes, pointy ears, and puzzled head tilt.

"Okey-dokey, Smoky," I said, and we finished the journey home together.

As we rounded the corner of the house, there was Mac rocking and puffing on his pipe.

"Well, Raymond, I got two pots going inside on the stove. The stew is for tonight. There's beans and bacon in the other pot, and there's bread there so feed yerselves while I go into the shop."

At that moment, I couldn't decide who I loved more, Smoky or Mac. I was starving.

I poured some beans into bowls for Smoky and me and looked around Mac's kitchen while I ate. His old farmhouse dated back almost to Confederation. The trap door to the cellar, with its earth walls and damp smells . . . the old furniture with all the secret compartments, and the big black stove.

Yet Mac liked to spend his time in the blacksmith shop over by the road, even though it had been closed since long before I was born. Mac's father used to run the shop, and he was a really smart man who also helped everyone around with their letters and taxes and wills. He taught Mac how to do a lot of the paperwork. Mom said Mac learned more about reading and writing and figuring from his father than he did in school.

Mac's father died when Mac was still young, and the shop closed down because nobody needed blacksmiths anymore, but that only made Mac funnier.

"I keep looking for a job but I just can't find anything in my line of work," he'd say.

Although the shop had been locked up forever, Mac would spend half his days in there. He kept a chain with a padlock on the front door, and the big sliding doors at the side were bolted shut. Brian, Billy, and I were able to crawl in through the floor on the gully side where it was all rotted. One time, Billy was bound and determined to ring the bell on the top floor, and Mac heard it and went bullshit. We never did it again, that's for sure.

"It's my business, buckos. You being in my business is a bit of a bother, you hear me? Stay out." Later, he said to me quietly, "It's where I settle my mind, Raymond."

I was always wondering what Mac did over there in the shop, so after breakfast I left Smoky in the farmhouse and wandered out to peek in one of the shop windows to see what he was up to. I changed windows until I could see him sitting at the long workbench where he couldn't see me. The shop was filled with thousands of oddments that Mom kept saying we should get around to organizing.

"Never do today what you can put off until it's unnecessary," Mac would say.

Even the workbench was covered with dozens of old tools, like someone had put them down yesterday and would be using them tomorrow. But Mac was paying no attention to tools. He had his steel-rimmed glasses hooked over his ears, and he was writing something on paper that was spread out across a big book that I knew he called his ledger. I watched him shuffle some loose papers like he was trying to find something, and then he'd write again. A couple of times he reached down into a big, black, wooden box on the floor that had a padlock hanging on it to pull out some more papers.

I wondered if it was a diary, but there seemed to be so much of it that its spread covered half the bench. After watching him for ten minutes and realizing he wasn't doing much, I got bored and wandered across the road to the grove of graves.

"The government gave them this land for nothing, over a hundred years ago," Mac said about the dead people. "You can't stick a fork in the ground without hitting a rock. If you get farmland for free, you pay for it with your life, and the life of everyone who comes behind you."

The grove of graves was overgrown with trees, sumac, and other bushes, and even poison ivy. Old hay and weeds covered the flat gravestones. Other gravestones had fallen over and were muddled through the trees, and that was another thing Mac was real crabby about. He had fought with the church because they wouldn't take care of this graveyard like they took care of the one up the hill. "Perpetual care don't last long, Raymond."

Mac said the graves here traced back to those who came across the Atlantic on the wretched coffin ships during Black '47, the famine in Ireland. He said that between these graves and the ones up the hill, the dead folks in Martindale outnumbered the live ones a hundred to one.

I loved this old graveyard. I could sit in the trees on a gravestone, hidden from view, and look across at the porch where Mac would yell at all the people passing by.

On Sundays, Mac and his ghastly goitre would perch on his rocker like a gargoyle, peering down the road at those coming up to church and peering up at God in St. Martin's steeple.

But most Sundays, when everyone was up at church, Mac would get his big scythe and bring me the small hand one, and we'd work in the old graveyard. We'd try to cut back the mess of stuff, and brush off the flat gravestones, and straighten the crooked ones. Half the time, Mac would be cursing the church for abandoning the graveyard, and the rest of the time, he'd be telling me his stories.

When the church bell started to ring at the end of Mass,

Mac would hustle us back across the road to sit at our post on the porch, so when everyone was leaving church they'd be reminded that Mac hadn't moved from his rocker and hadn't done anything useful all the time they'd been at Mass.

"We wouldn't want to be seen working on the Lord's day of rest. It'd be a sin," Mac would say and he'd sit and rock until each and every car and wagon and all the walkers had gone back down the hill.

"It'd be better if they'd spend their time with us in the graveyard. Not up there listening to Father Foley. Any God he could understand wouldn't be much of a God."

I could have sat there in the graveyard thinking peacefully for half the day, but that's when Mac shouted, "Raymond, I'll get my gun and you get Smoky. We're gone to find a zombie."

We started up the hill. Smoky was running ahead and behind and around, smelling and pissing on everything. Smoky would stick to me like a burr when we were alone together, but when we were both with him he'd circle from one of us to the other like a pesky fly. Mac had his gun. He brought it everywhere. It was a little rifle, a single-shot .22.

The gun was another reason everyone thought Mac was crazy. Brian told me that Billy told him that one time Mac trudged up the hill when everyone was already at Mass praying hard. That first time in the Mass when the priest turns to face the congregation and says *"Dominus vobiscum,"* and then the congregation responds with, *"Et cum spiritu tuo"* — at that moment Father Foley was staring right down the centre aisle at Mac, who was standing just inside the big back doors with the rifle hanging from his armpit and staring right back at Father Foley, who froze with *"Oremus"* locked in his throat. (Usually, once Foley *"Oremus*ed" and turned back toward the altar, Billy and his friends, who sat in the back row, knew they had more than twelve minutes before Foley would turn to view his parishioners again. That was plenty of time to sneak out for a smoke.)

Anyway, there was Mac standing with his big ugly grin,

but by the time the others wondered about Foley's frozen death stare and turned to see what he was looking at, Mac was gone.

When I asked Mac about it, he just said, "Don't worry. I never shoot the meek or the mild."

It was true that Mac didn't shoot much except for groundhogs and tin cans. He wasn't a hunter. He wouldn't shoot at a bird, and he loved crows because they had saved his life. That's another story Mac told that made folks think he was crazy. There was an abandoned well beside the back barn, and when Mac tried to fix it, he fell in. He told everyone that he was down there for a long while watching the crows fly around the top of the well.

Then it started to get dark.

"I knew I was a goner," Mac said. "I was clinging to a small rise in the mud, my bottom half was in the water and frozen, and I was going to conk out. The crows were making one hell of a fuss, and then a rope tumbles down on me. I pulled till it was taut, crawled myself to the top, and there's the rope tied to a tree. No one there except for the crows. A million of them. All staring down and cawing at me from the two big pines. I was so tuckered I could only lie on my back, look up, and pray to my black friends."

On the way up the hill, Mac told me he'd seen the zombie on other nights, too, as if coming out of the church.

"I done some snoopin' while you were sweatin' and stookin'. Trying to find out why the zombie has been hanging around Upper Low so much and where he may be livin'."

By this time, we were at the front of the church at the top of Martindale Hill. Mac tried the doors on each side of the entrance. They were locked. He knew they'd be locked but it was his ritual every time he passed. He told everyone that a church—which they all knew he never went to—should always be open to the faithful.

"Well, Raymond. The zombie can't be running in and out of the church, that's for sure."

Just then, Father Foley came across from the priest's house, his black soutane swishing, and holding his pendant crucifix like a pistol.

"Something I can do for you, Mac?"

"You're keepin' her locked up pretty good, Father. Expecting thieves?"

"Not with you down there keeping a watch on everything." I could see Father Foley's eyes looking down at Mac's gun.

"Father, I've been meaning to talk to you about one of the dead folks across the way."

"They're all dead across the way, Mac."

Mac cackled, "An oldie but goodie, Father." That seemed to relax the good Father a bit.

"His name was Mondou. That's sort of like 'My God' in French, is it not? A saintly name, to be sure. I know of the Field-ville family by that name but I don't remember anything about this Alfred fella dying. When was that? There's no date of death on the gravestone."

Father Foley hesitated a moment.

"A year or two back. A man so young. The family took it hard. They haven't gotten around to filling in the date. You must have been away when he died, Mac."

Even I knew that Mac was never away, but just then Father Foley changed the subject.

"I want to talk to you about across the way, Mac. It's a Catholic cemetery. You're still running your jalopy around in there, and I want it to stop. I've told you before, it's dangerous." Mac used his jalopy only when he wanted to get to a far place at a certain time, because he wasn't much of a driver.

"Who am I gonna kill in a cemetery, Father?"

"It's sanctified ground, Mac. It must stop."

"All right, Father. It was a good place to practise but I can drive her well enough now anyway."

"You'll have to come up to church without your gun, Mac."

"I'll do that for your wedding, Father."

I laughed out loud. Father Foley gave me such a look.

Then as Mac was turning to leave, he saw Marian. She was the priest's cook and maid. She was wearing wildflowers in her hair, sitting on the lawn with her little girl, and smiling her cozy smile and waving.

Mac turned back to Father Foley.

"I'll not bring my gun up when I come for the baptism of your child, either, Father." Mac was staring hard at Father Foley when he said it. Father Foley was staring back like an avenging angel. I had to look away.

"Old Mac, you are scandalizing the young, and me, and Holy Mother Church. That will place you in the deepest part of hell."

But Mac had already turned and started up the road. He didn't seem to care about the deepest part of hell, but it scared the shit out of me.

When I caught up with him he said, "I think I'll be a small fry in the deepest part of hell, don't you, Raymond? Foley should spend more time in the Herenow instead of in the Hereafter."

But I was busy thinking about Marian's little girl and how Mom and Gertie talked about it when I was at my listening post. Some said the father of Marian's little girl, and the next kid she was about to have, was Father Foley. Others had other guesses, and some even said it was Old Mac, because they seemed to like each other so much. That used to make my mom and Gertie laugh like crazy, too.

One night at my listening post, I heard Mac say to Proulx, "The little girl looks French. I'm putting my money on Père Beaubien, but you'll never get that out of Foley. Those two are thicker than thieves."

That was another time Proulx screamed French curses at Mac and left swearing that he'd never come back.

With all that thinking about Marian, I blurted out, "Marian has the nicest smile I've ever seen, Mac."

Mac didn't break stride. "You're right about that, Raymond. She's radiant. You were going to look that word up in the dictionary."

"I did, Mac. It means rays of light and energy, beaming with joy, and dazzling, and stuff like that."

"Well, that's all true, don't you think?"

"Yep."

We turned off before O'Sullivan's farmhouse and headed down to the river on a road that was only a couple of ruts, with Smoky still peeing on everything. He never ran out.

As we approached the bush that ran along the river, it smelled like burnt hay and pine, and the sky ran up into a bunch of blues and over there were all the places I could someday be.

Suddenly Mac stopped by the wire fence that ran along the road and pointed at the cows grazing in the field under the hydro lines. The hydro lines were new. Mac said that ever since they went up a year ago, the cows were different.

"They used to stand around all pretty well facing in the same direction," he said. "Now they face in all different directions, like they don't know where they're going. I think that electricity running just over their heads is frying their brains for sure." He bent over to pull some dewy grass and put it in his mouth and started to chew it like the cow that was chewing its cud right in front of us. I did the same thing.

After a while, Mac said, "Well, Raymond, whadda we got?"

That was my cue.

"We got the Herenow and the Hereafter." Then we both sang out together,

"And we're not sure of the Hereafter."

The cow didn't even blink.

Then we walked down the road singing "The Bum Song." I felt like Dorothy dancing down the yellow brick road with the scarecrow. Smoky was running beside us like he was Toto.

When we'd finished singing, I asked, "Where are we going, Mac?"

"We're going where we shouldn't go, to see what we shouldn't see, and where I think a zombie could hide. O'Sullivan's Island is not far up the river from the church with bush and gullies on it. I heard a rumour that the island was serving some folks well. The zombie has to be somewhere."

Yeah, in a coffin in a graveyard, I was thinking, but I was thrilled to be on the adventure, too. I felt like Captain Marvel.

Mac often joked about how I was invincible. He even made me look up the word in the dictionary, and I memorized the definition and would say it over and over again like a prayer whenever I was scared. As a baby, I had slipped off the upstairs bed and slid through the heat hole down to the floor below. After bouncing off magazines on a stand I sat there on the floor in my diapers. Mac said I was laughing when he picked me up, but that the ladies raced down the stairs screaming so much they finally scared me into crying.

Then when I was five, I got lost in the bush but wandered home in the dark, and then had to sit on the porch until everyone came back from looking for me. And early that summer, when a horse bolted, I rolled a hay wagon and was thrown clear of the whole mess. Uncle Martin wouldn't let me run the rig again, which made Billy think I'd done the whole thing on purpose.

Just then we came up over the rise where the ruts turned to a path that led down to the river. Smoky charged down the hill, ran out on the little dock, and leaped into the water. None of my yelling did any good.

"He'll be learning about the current up by here any time now," Mac said. Dogs could be dumb sometimes.

Sure enough, Smoky figured he'd better paddle like hell if he was going to get back to the shore, which he did about fifty yards down. He dried himself with his wet-dog shake, came up the shore to the dock and jumped into the little rowboat with us, cool as a cucumber.

Now I was worried. If we ran into zombies, I was invincible. But Smoky might fight, and Mac was old.

I knew that if we got into zombie trouble, Mac would try to talk himself out of it. Problem was, the zombies I'd seen in movies weren't very good listeners.

SIX

December 1944

"WILLIAMS SHOULD BE doing this, Mondou. Not me," Sergeant Dolan said. "But he told me if he got you into a room alone, he'd probably kill you. He really loved your JAP project, and he liked you. He bragged about you. Claimed you were great at making things happen. I guess you made the wrong things happen."

Dolan leaned back and laughed loud at his own joke.

"So it's simple, really. We're laying charges against the lot of you. Lots of them. So far there are 171 charges. Seems like there are more against you than the others. Let's see. Theft of military weapons, kidnapping, issuing armed threats . . ."

Mondou flashed Dolan a vicious look.

"I stopped the mutiny."

"Yes, well. That's the minority opinion, Mondou. Williams doesn't see it that way. He warned you not to go in there. Many of your mutineer friends say it was all your idea in the first place. You were the idea man. Like Trotsky or Marx or something. Personally, I think the mutiny ended because those jellyfish quitters got hungry. Then they had the shit scared out of them by one phony barrage. It had nothing to do with you."

Dolan looked at the single piece of paper sitting on the desk in front of him.

"It gets worse, Mondou. A file folder just arrived from HQ in

Ottawa. Personnel is going over it now. There are some charges here filed by a Corporal Grafftey. He called up when he saw the communique with your name mentioned. He says to say hello, by the way. Says he never transmitted the charges before to give you a break at your new base. Start off on the right foot and all that."

Dolan glanced up.

"Apparently, you were trying to do the same thing in Petawawa. There's some good stuff here." Dolan raised his eyes and fixed them again on Mondou. Nothing. "Anyway, you can view all of this as 'no good deed goes unpunished,' but personally I see it as 'all's well that ends well.' You and your Pepsi friends got little press and zero sympathy but you have managed to piss off a lot of important people. We're volunteering you and your comrades to Active status, which we're now allowed to do. So, as I said, for you it's simple, really. Spend the rest of your life in the brig or take your chances in battle. Go and kill some Germans, for Christ's sake."

As Dolan thundered through his kill line, there was knocking on the door. Dolan went to the door, stepped out for a few moments, and came back with another officer.

"Mondou, you know Corporal James from Personnel." They nodded to each other as James went and stood by the wall. "James wants to ask you a few questions."

James extracted a file folder from his armpit and opened it.

"Mondou. This file contains some charges against you and all of your background records, but there's another notification. Were you ever told that your mother passed away about . . . ahh, let's see . . . maybe two months ago?"

Mondou swallowed with difficulty. His mind was racing. Someone would have written. His sisters, brother. But Mère wrote all the letters in the family, and he hadn't had a response to his last letter.

"It's a mistake," he said.

"Well, this notification is from a priest. It's in French, but

I'm told it serves as an official death notice in Quebec. Seems to be a Père Beaubien."

The tears were all inside and starting to gag Mondou.

Mère was dead.

"No one told me."

"You have my sympathies, Mondou. But this changes nothing," Dolan interrupted. "You'll leave the day after tomorrow. You won't catch up with the first batch of zombies being shipped out of Halifax, but you'll be close behind. We need you over there."

Mondou just sat and stared at him. If he'd been in prison, he thought, he would have been told about Mère's death and been allowed to go to her funeral.

Dolan stood up and was edging toward the door. "Who knows," he said. "You might like the fight. I think you'll be good at it."

Mondou had too much time to think about his mother during the four-day train trip to Montreal. He and the others were totally confined to their car, unlike the more casual troop movement west three years earlier. Almost two hundred of them were transported in three rail cars that were constructed as cages to ensure that they all reached their destination.

Mondou's wandering would not have been welcomed anyway. Most of the conscripts would not talk to him. He could only imagine that Jacques and his friends blamed him for the failure of the mutiny, because Onesime was hurling insults in Mondou's direction without acknowledging that he was even there.

"Mondou is the fucking reason we're all off to war. Just remember that."

Mondou sat alone by the window, and no one came to join him.

His work at Terrace had been a good delaying action. It kept the future away. Now he could see that there were no good outcomes. Just go to war and die, or get home when it was too late. Mère was already dead, his sisters surely inconsolable, and his brother handling the stress in the worst possible way. His family and all of Fieldville must have been confused by Mondou's absence at the funeral.

He considered his position. He could go to war with those sitting around him, who hated him, wouldn't talk to him, and happened to be piss-poor soldiers, and never get back to his fractured family.

Or he could place his hope in Duplessis. Quebec City had just vowed to stop Ottawa from shipping zombies to Europe, and the Duplessis November 30th Order-in-Council was now the talk of the train.

Someone shouted, "We won't be shipped past Val Cartier. Just watch."

Mondou did not want to watch any longer. From Montreal, they'd be trained to Halifax and shipped to Europe.

He could do something about that. Thus far in his life, when he was making things happen, he was happy. When he let things happen, the results were disastrous.

He'd get off the goddamned train before it reached Montreal and disappear into the mountains.

Through the silence of his final night on the train, he studied the memory map in his mind. He knew it was best to desert the train after it passed the border into Quebec but before it reached Montreal. He knew the area just west of Montreal well. Beyond that, he'd be lost. He estimated that between Saint-Zotique and Montreal's train station, he had about a fifty-mile window.

The next day, they were approaching Montreal in the late afternoon, and Mondou had not yet seen his opportunity. He began to fear that he'd have to make his break from the centre of a city he had never seen.

He was still sitting silently by the window in the last seat at the east end of the car with no one beside him. The only times he had moved were to stretch in the aisle, or to access the washroom beyond the cage under the watchful eye of the corporal guard who sat in the one row between the cage and the end of the car. When they had stopped at stations, there was always a CN policeman stationed in the vestibule between the cars.

Alfred listened again for the patterns he'd been hearing for four days. Near Dorval, the train started shunting into a slower mode for the final approach into Montreal. He heard the CN policeman in the vestibule between the cars unlock the top half of the big side door, and then lock it into place against the end wall. If he could get out, there was a space of four square feet that he could climb through and then leap from the train.

The problem was the locked cage just beyond his right elbow.

Now with only minutes to Central Station, everyone seemed to be preparing for arrival. The corporal guard behind Mondou stood up, put on his overcoat, and proceeded to unlock the cage door.

Mondou couldn't believe it when the corporal started to walk the full length of the rail car with a chain of keys in hand. He clearly thought his job was done. The cargo had been delivered to Montreal.

Mondou had to move fast so that even his comrades would have no time to raise an alarm. He left his small satchel underneath the seat, ignored his coat on the overhead rack, turned low, saw no one through the window in the vestibule and carefully started to open the door to the loud clatter and squeal of the shifting train.

The CN policeman had just removed the bottom door of the vestibule and was standing on the stairs leaning out to look forward down the tracks when he glimpsed someone behind him.

It was too late.

Mondou looked at the one remaining obstacle between him

and freedom. He anchored himself with his arms on the lift rails and swung his boots.

The guard flew from the train, flailing into the air. Mondou moved to the bottom step. He took a quick look forward, then leapt as far from the train as he could.

The impact was far worse than he expected, and he found himself rolling more than he thought possible. He finally slammed up against a signal pole and stopped. The train had already passed well beyond him, so it was going much faster than he thought when he jumped. He got to his feet and stood there stretching and searching for pain but there was none. He smiled to himself, while standing knee-deep in the banks of recently fallen snow.

"Merci Dieu."

The whole episode had taken no more than a minute. It was time for a new sense of urgency. He started moving across the tracks to the south. As soon as the embankment permitted, he crawled up out of the railway cut with the thought of finding the highway that he knew as the "2 & 20."

It was December, and the sun was setting, and before long it would be very, very cold. Mondou wanted to get as far away from the scene of his escape as possible. The army had taught him to march more than twenty miles a day. He didn't have to carry a thirty-pound packsack, so he could get to Vaudreuil well before midnight, but he intended to get farther than that before he slept again. If he could walk through the night, he knew a place where he might sleep through the next day and then continue his journey.

Day was slipping into darkness as Mondou crawled out of the railway cut and ran across Highway 2 & 20. He felt sure people were wondering why the man in army fatigues was running along the side of the highway. He had to get a civilian overcoat for camouflage and for warmth before he started west.

On the south side of the highway, he tried to stay in the deepening shadows as he marched quickly to the corner of

Bouchard and Martin avenues. He gazed down Martin, which was empty and bordered by small homes. Far down at the foot of the street, he could see a pale flashing light.

It seemed less than half a mile south.

When he reached the corner, he saw the Hotel de Dorval. The side door was open and inside was the hubbub of Happy Hour and the smell of stale beer. When he heard laughter approaching, he quickly retreated to the Women's, probably the quietest place in the hotel at five p.m. He heard a few men fumble with galoshes and coats, and once their voices blended in with the sounds from the main lounge, he headed to the coatroom. He reached for the longest, largest overcoat and then exited out the side entrance. In the coat pockets, he found a pair of leather mitts. Back on Lakeshore, he started walking west at a forced-march pace.

By midnight, he was twenty miles away in the Vaudreuil Inn, standing with his back against the wall near the entrance, drinking in the smoke and uproarious laughter mixed with *franglais* vulgarity. There was probably not a sober person in the room, which was the best that he could hope for.

Mondou was jubilant. He was back in a familiar place for the first time since being shipped out of Hull to Camp Petawawa almost three years ago. He could even see the table that he and his father had sat at ten years earlier.

Suddenly, a big, bouncing waitress charged through the dim clouds.

"*Une bière, monsieur?*" He had no money to buy beer, but he couldn't admit to that.

He shook his head. "*Non, merci.*"

A moment later, he saw the waitress at a table, and everyone in the bar seemed to be turning to have a look at the stranger who stood in bars but wouldn't drink. He could quickly become the floor show, which was not good.

A French shout came from one of the tables. "Monsieur, join us for a beer." They were making an attempt to be friendly, and Mondou knew he had to respond. He walked over, stood by one of the several tables that were giving him their undivided attention, and responded in the French that would betray him as a local.

"I would love to join you, believe me, but I must find a way to get to Hawkesbury tonight because of a serious family matter."

They all understood serious family matters.

"There's only one *maudit* crazy enough to head for Hawkesbury tonight," one man shouted. Then he whacked a short fat man at the next table. "Gilles, you said you wanted to make it to Montpetit's tonight?" Montpetit was the name of the Hawkesbury Hotel that the Montebello workers frequented regularly. Mondou knew it well.

Gilles, with his forehead almost on the table, blubbered that he had to get home because he must be at work in the morning or Lise would remove his genitals.

"We have a stranger here who wants you to drive him to Hawkesbury, Gilles. Wake up, *tabernac*."

Mondou introduced himself to Gilles as Philippe and wasted no time helping him up from the table. Gilles reached out to grab his glass to bring it with him. Mondou steered him toward the door and out to the parking lot. They exited to peals of laughter surrounding the proposal of a toast. Mondou knew they were toasting the poor stranger who would have to be driven down Highway 17 by the drunken Gilles.

Gilles pointed to his car. Mondou negotiated the keys from his hand and put Gilles in the passenger seat, and Gilles was too focused on not spilling his beer to resist. Mondou couldn't believe his luck.

Twenty-two miles and less than forty minutes later, he was parking Gilles's car near the front entrance of the Hawkesbury Hotel. He put the keys back in the man's pocket and started him staggering through the foyer into the noisy tavern room, knowing he would never remember how he had gotten to

Montpetit's.

Mondou then walked out of the parking lot, jogged slowly through Hawkesbury, and across the Perley Bridge back into Quebec. He was now on home ground but he still had a fifteen-mile hike before he could sleep. The snow was deeper here, but he could walk on the road where it was hard-packed. There was no traffic. All he could hear was the crunch-squeak of his boots on the snow.

He had forgotten how beautiful it was on a crisp, cloud-less night with a sky full of moon and stars. Every tree, hill, gully, and outbuilding was covered in snow, reflecting light and shadow. All of it brightened the air in a way that magnified the magic.

He turned, walked backwards often, and scanned the horizon constantly. He did not want to be surprised by a vehicle. If he saw headlights he would leap over the tall roadside snow-banks into the ditch. He did not want to explain himself to someone offering a lift or, worse yet, talk to a policeman.

But it seemed even drunks weren't out at one a.m. on a Tuesday. He found himself not only walking backwards for stretches but twirling and strutting and skipping. He was in his place, and happy. Always in sight there was a farmhouse, and every one displayed multicoloured Christmas lights. Some had a crèche under a tree near the front porch.

The Christmas season had always been important to Mondou. No other time of year was nearly so wonderful. The midnight Mass on Christmas Eve was a mélange of Latin and traditional carols sung by the cantor and the choir. Mondou had been in the choir with a dozen other boys and older women since he was very young.

When the Mass was over, each family would walk up to the crèche to visit the infant Jesus lying in his manger. Mondou's father had sculpted the baby Jesus himself. It was considered an honour. Mondou had carved one of the gentle cows. They would greet all the other parishioners, and all those who were back from the city for Christmas. His father would pull up the big sleigh and they would head home at two p.m. for the *reveillon*, the first meal of Les Fêtes. Thick logs burned on the fire as they sat down to a groaning board of cretons, ragout, tourtière, cranberries cooked in maple syrup, mashed potatoes, pickled vegetables, donuts, and *tarte au sucre*.

Mondou's daydreaming made him realize that he was not only very happy to be home but also very hungry. Of course, he would not get to eat tonight, and it would not be that kind of Christmas ever again. The police would be close behind. They knew where he meant to go.

By 2:45 a.m., he had snuck onto the grounds at Montebello, slid quietly in the back door of the horse stables, climbed the ladder to the loft, removed his stolen overcoat to use as a blanket, and lain down in the hay in the same place he used to sleep when he worked at the Chateau.

He was back home, and his soul was back in his body.

He would never leave again. They'd have to kill him first.

SEVEN

August 1947

We untied the old rowboat and rowed out into the current that would take us downstream to the island, trying to avoid all the timber in the river. Mac was doing more looking than rowing.

"Raymond. I have me here a riddle. What can you only see from the middle?" He was peering around in a funny way like a lighthouse, trying to give me a clue, I think.

"A river."

"Right," Mac roared, and he doffed his hat in my direction. "Especially this river. Look around. There's no other way to see it. It's wooded to both shores. Not a path on either side."

Mac found an opening through the huge rocks that surrounded the island, and Smoky leapt out as we dragged the boat onto a rocky ledge. I looked up and shivered. Tall trees formed a thick, dark layer that seemed to surround everything else.

Mac started to walk.

"I know my bush and already this one looks busy," he muttered. "See the old bushes, brambles, and ferns all flat? Small trees busted up here and here?"

We walked uphill for a bit and soon we were looking down onto a large, round gully. I was thinking it seemed a good place to hide.

I followed Mac down into the gully, and right across the clearing to another path that took us clear through to the rocks on the other side of the island. Mac knelt down and touched some ruts that led down to the rocks.

"That's what they could be up to."

"Who, zombies?"

"Maybe, but there must have been a lot of them."

We'd be outnumbered for sure.

Mac headed back to the gully clearing and looked left and right.

"They sure cleared enough to see what was coming from the four corners. Nothing here is fresh, but it was very busy here *not long ago*. You go left, I'll go right."

I really didn't want to be alone but I headed left. I was relieved when Smoky decided to come with me.

I didn't know what I was looking for but I found it. Smoky was running ahead sniffing everything and he found an old cigarette pack beside a big flat rock like the rocks down on the shore. Something was carved on the rock.

It was the same symbol that was on the gravestone. Except the Z was in red. Like blood.

I ran like hell to get Mac.

I found him down on his hands and knees.

"Lookee here. A shell casing. This isn't for any gun in these parts. Assault rifle of some kind. Army gear."

"I've got something better, Mac. Over there."

When he saw it, he just kept shaking his head back and forth.

"Well, hell. You're right, Raymond. We'll have to look at that grave again on the way back. This makes a big difference!"

"What difference can one letter make, Mac?"

"It's a symbol, a message, a code, lots of things. Look how a jumble of twenty-six letters has given us every book in the language. Even one letter is a lot. Think of the 'Z,' Raymond."

Zombie. I shuddered.

We kept looking around for quite a while and found more rubbish.

"It's been busier than downtown Ottawa around these parts, and they're just as messy as city folk."

"The zombies?"

"Or whoever was chasing them. Fugitives would be more careful. The zombies were probably using the island, poaching, and then there was an army of folks out here."

What were the zombies poaching? Brains?

Before long, we rowed back, tied up the boat, and headed home. On Martindale Road we ran into Barry O'Sullivan coming across his field.

"Remember what I told you, Raymond," Mac whispered to me, and then he shouted, "Hi, there, Barry O. I'd like you to meet my great-nephew, Raymond."

"Doesn't look like there's too much great about him."

Mac answered, "Don't be insulting, Barry. Raymond is a right smart lad."

"Hi, there, Raymond. My name is Barry **O**'Sullivan." He said the letter "O" real long and strong. "But folks just call me Barry O. I guess you're wondering about the O."

I nodded, because Mac had warned me to listen to Barry about the O, because Barry loved the story so much.

"A couple of hundred years ago back in Ireland, there were no Sullivans, just O'Sullivans. Well it turns out that some of the O'Sullivans got pretty rich while the other O'Sullivans stayed dirt poor. Then the rich O'Sullivans got pretty fancy and they didn't want anyone thinking they were related to the poor O'Sullivans. So they went to all the poor O'Sullivans and said, 'We'll buy your 'O.' You change your name to Sullivan and we'll pay you a princely sum.' And you know what my dear old forefathers did?"

"What?"

"They said no. That's what they did. When all the others were selling their 'O,' my clan wouldn't sell. Our ancestors told us to never allow anyone to change our name, and nobody has messed with us since. We're proud O'Sullivans and we will be until the end of time."

I didn't think much of the story, and I wondered whether his O'Sullivan forefathers should have sold their 'O,' since they had a lot of other letters in their name.

"Who's doing the camping out on your island, Barry?" Mac asked.

"I don't get back there too much so I don't know what's going on. I did notice a newer camp out there a while back, but no sign of them going by from here. I had a look, though. I think they're Frogs, and I think I know what they're up to."

"And what's that?"

"They're poaching Eddy's logs and running them somewhere. There's good money in that. But they must work from the other side of the river. E.B. Eddy must know about it, though. Some QPP came snooping around, but nothing came of it."

Mac seemed to absorb this news slowly. "Think it's a gang of zombies, Barry?"

I froze, but Mac's question didn't seem to bother Barry at all.

"Oh, I don't believe all them old zombie stories. Just local legends. If there had been any wandering around, they'd have disappeared after the war."

"And where on earth would they disappear to? Most people around know that the QPP were not going to much trouble to find them, and the RCMP and army only took one or two shots at it, so if they didn't want to turn themselves in, they could still be out there."

Barry just shrugged. They were talking about zombies like they were just wandering around everywhere all the time.

"These zombie fellas have been skulking around for a long while now," Mac said. "It's time that stuff was over."

Barry looked at him and laughed.

"Mac, I thought you'd love the zombies. They're not ploughing and reaping and haying and stooking. If they're there, they're hunting and poaching, buying and selling, and feasting and fighting. And the folks that think they're around seem to envy them, as far as I can see."

Mac thought for a minute. "Yeah, and if folks heard they were going to be hanged tomorrow there'd be twice as many as envy them who'd be down to see it."

Why hang a zombie if it's already dead? I wondered. I was also thinking Barry O. was right. Sounded like the zombies had the kind of adventures that Mac would like. As we walked along, Mac started another ditty.

> "We seek him here, we seek him there,
> We seek the zombie everywhere.
> Is he in heaven or is he in hell,
> His Gatineau ghouls will never tell."

"You know your uncle's crazy, don't ya," Barry whispered to me. "You'd better figure out how to get him to mind his own business."

I didn't answer. I did know Mac was probably crazy but I didn't like Barry saying so.

I didn't know how Mac became so different. Maybe it was because he didn't have a job or hardly went to school, like an old Huck Finn. One thing I knew was that all that investigating and nosing into things meant every day was an adventure, and that seemed enough for Mac. Every day was just another tune played on his harmonica.

And I sure didn't know how to get Mac to mind his own business. Nobody did. Low was like all other places. Certain things were known, and other things were not. I guess Mac wanted to know everything there was to know in the Gatineau, and there was no stopping him.

We said goodbye to O'Sullivan and headed back down the road toward Martindale.

"Raymond," Mac said, "Barry O. has just been telling us

some real whoppers. He knows his land like the back of his hand. There's half a city out on his small island, and suddenly he don't know which way the wind is blowing. Sometimes I think I'm either goin' crazy or everyone in the Gatineau is trying to bamboozle me. Or I'm Rip Van Winkle. I fell asleep and missed the whole thing. I don't give a damn if they all think I'm crazy. I just don't want them thinking I'm stupid. Do you think I'm crazy?"

I was just going to answer that I didn't care if he was crazy or not, but Mac interrupted by doing his loopty-loop with an elbow up over his ear then pressing a thumb and finger to each side of his nose just above the nostrils and shotgunning mucus onto the gravel. If he wasn't doing that, he was squirting tobacco juice. I was usually ready for both because I didn't want to be cleaning snot or spit off Smoky. Then Mac would take out his handkerchief and wipe the rest of his very large nose. It was as if he didn't want to dirty his handkerchief on the major part of the job.

We stopped at the graveyard on our way back, and Mac studied the Mondou gravestone. It was like I had said. There was a Z on the gravestone running from the bottom of the P. It sure wasn't an X.

Mac stood there and stared at it for what seemed like a long time.

"Well, me bucko. It's Saturday night. It's time to head to Low, have some craic, and find out just who's dead and who's undead."

We headed down the hill from the cemetery, and I was thinking again that maybe I should have headed back to Ottawa, where the only zombies were the ones in the movies.

EIGHT

December 1944

MONDOU HAD REACHED Lac Ste. Marie, where he was living in a cottage he had broken into. He knew the difference between the chalets that were sometimes used for skiing, and the summer cottages that were abandoned for the winter. He chose one that was well back from the lake on a snow-covered, dead-end road. He used the small fireplace only after proving to himself that the smoke wasn't easily detectable from the town across the lake.

He ransacked the cottage and found some old dungarees and shirts with paint on them. He had managed to steal some small amounts of money from the local church and some food in town, but he knew that he'd have to get much better organized. He needed a gun to shoot small game, and transportation.

He also needed more money, and much more information.

It turned out it wasn't that difficult to get information about his family by eavesdropping on the local gossip. It seemed the Mondous of Fieldville, although far away, were a popular subject because they had fallen on hard times, and there was nothing the locals liked talking about more than other folks' hard times.

"After the father died and P'tit went west, the family went into the shitter. The three sisters aren't yet to the altar, and that Marc likes his whiskey more than his milking. And now

Alfred's dead in that train accident. Killed a cop, they say . . ."

Mondou remembered the guard that he had pushed from the train. What was his own status with the authorities? How did he go about returning to a normal life after his wasted years in Terrace? How could he even communicate with his family? What kind of family was left?

He was angry—at the army, the government. He couldn't even help his remaining family. He couldn't work the farm, or anywhere else for that matter. There were all of the original charges from Terrace and his escape and God knows what else.

That's when the idea struck him.

By reading the bulletin on the vestibule wall of the church in Lac Ste. Marie, Mondou confirmed that Père Beaubien was still pastor in the area, and that he would be in the church at four p.m. the next Saturday—the last Saturday before Christmas.

Father Beaubien was in his usual confessional coma behind the screen in the dark when he heard a name that startled him awake.

"*Au nom du Père, du Fils, et du Saint Esprit.* Bless me, Father, for I have sinned. I confess to Almighty God and to you, Père. My name is Alfred Mondou, and these are my sins."

"*C'est qui?* You are who?"

"Alfred Mondou."

Beaubien turned and peered through the screen. Despite the beard, it was indeed Alfred Mondou. Beaubien broke into a big grin and started to rise to leave the confessional.

"*Non*, Père. Please stay. I need to talk to you in the confidence of the confessional," said Mondou.

"I understand, my son. And I need to talk to you. But if it is a long talk, the busybodies out there will get much too interested in the big sinner in the confessional box. Leave the confessional now, and kneel to say your penance as usual, and then go by the back door into the house. I will be there soon. I have so much to tell you."

"I'll be there, Père. Take your time. I have nowhere else to go."

"The prodigal son returns," Beaubien chuckled to himself.

In the priest's house, Mondou told Père everything, from "storming the Bastille" to stealing money from his church. Beaubien seemed mostly entertained by it all. Then Beaubien told Mondou just about everything he needed to know. The most important piece of information was that he was most definitely wanted by the police, and there was no shortage of charges, including the charge of murder. The CN policeman that Mondou had pushed from the train had indeed died of his severe injuries.

Mondou groaned. Beaubien almost seemed annoyed by the interruption.

"There are worse sins than yours, Mondou. You have not abandoned your faith, and are still part of Holy Mother, the Church. And you have not committed the mortal sin of murder. It was an accident, that's all. A venial sin, perhaps. In any case, *ego te absolvo.*" And with that, Père threw Mondou an air blessing and continued as if Mondou had simply confessed to the sin of masturbation.

Beaubien went on to tell Alfred that his family in Fieldville had already been visited by authorities from the Department of National Defence together with the QPP. They had searched the area for Mondou and left his brother and sisters with threats of reprisals if they did not turn him in. Père could not explain the rumours of his death but he had heard them. He had already suggested to his brother Marc that he should be comforted by the hope that Alfred was still alive, since there had been no official notice of his death.

"I told him, 'Do not deny the death, Marc. The more people who believe your brother is dead, the more we will all be left alone.'"

Père then told Alfred about his mother's death.

"After your father died, your mother was never the same. You must have seen that. They were quite a pair, those two, and I loved them like family. You know your mother got weaker, and many thought it was only her grief. When you were taken away, it got very much worse, and we brought her to Barbee in Wakefield. They call everything they don't understand consumption, but it was cancer, according to Dr. Barbee. You can be sure that she's in heaven now."

"Did she know I wasn't here, near the end, Père?" Mondou asked.

"She knew you weren't here every minute you were gone, Alfred. She feared so much for you."

Beaubien assured Alfred that not only were the proper death notices served, but he himself had sent them to Defence head-quarters in Ottawa.

Père slammed his hand onto his armrest. "The army of England doesn't care about a French zombie's mother, Alfred. Even as a boy you had more strength of soul than anyone. *They* are the zombies."

Mondou suddenly felt very, very tired.

"Père, I have nowhere to go. No way to earn a living. My family needs help. I need to help them, but how? There will be no cheques from the army. If I had gone to their war—"

Beaubien suddenly stood up and took a harsher tone.

"If you had gone to their war, you'd be dead. If not dead then different in ways you cannot understand. In ways that would be of no help to your family. Your family is not too bad. I see to that. You must be strong, Alfred. You were always the strongest. Forget their damned war."

Père paused and cleared his throat. "Years ago, there were five Beaubien boys and five sisters near Saint-Jean-sur-Richelieu. We were a strong family, *beau et bien*. The two oldest, my brothers, were strong men and would take their rightful place as the lead-ers of *les Beaubiens*. They went to the war. The one they call the Great War. They were anxious to get away from the routine of the farm. As if they were off to some fête in France. After what the British had done to us, they were off to fight for an empire they knew nothing about. *Incroyable!*"

Père paused again. His voice grew louder.

"They were part of the Royal 22e Regiment that was head-quartered in Saint-Jean. Both were killed in France in the same battle. Sixty-five thousand Canadians died in that war. This young land lost all its young men. The world lost ten million young men, and twenty million were wounded, diseased, muti-lated, spitting blood. Twenty million civilians were killed. Many more were dead in their heads. Every one of them was a child of God. For what, Alfred? They died for what? So we do it all over again twenty years later." Père had gone from a severe tone to shouts, and back again.

"No Beaubien would ever live again as we did for one hundred years. I had become a priest. Phillippe had become a drunk and moved to Rhode Island with my youngest brother, Jean. *Mon père*, sick from his sadness, was fooled into selling his land for the uranium."

Père's eyes filled with tears.

"They called it the Great War. I call it the Great Waste. Such a great, great waste, Alfred. And now it is happening all over again. The same old empires in the same old Europe settling the same old scores, and now the poor Jews, and millions of innocents are caught up in it again. God's innocents,"

"Many say this is the Good War, Père."

"I have studied this good war. It is like all war. Wars of choice. The choice of a few men. The Hitler, the Stalin, and that Churchill, who has been part of both wars. If you want to under-stand the British and this man Churchill, learn about Dieppe, Alfred. Understand what the British and Churchill did to Canadi-ans at Dieppe, and you will understand evil. It was forced suicide. There are men who have a lust for war. And like all lust, they let it happen without prayer, without thought for the consequences or the innocents. Years from now, history will understand that a hundred million people suffered death and anguish during these two wars for nothing much. The first war was unnecessary, and the second its consequence. With a tragedy so enormous, what is the difference between victory and defeat? A hundred million lives ruined because of a few men. Believe me, the men who are the cause will spend eternity in hell, and Great Britain will no longer be great."

Alfred had heard this rant years before, sitting at the Mondou kitchen table. He realized that, like a war, Père would continue his argument until his opponent was subdued.

"I must agree, Père."

Père paused. He seemed to be calming himself.

"You missed their war. You can't catch up. You must look forward."

"Again, I agree."

"Do you want to leave the country? I have family in Rhode Island."

"I will never leave here again, Père. I'm prepared for them to kill me but I will die *chez nous.*"

"You could surrender and pray that the courts don't send you to prison."

Mondou just shook his head from side to side like a young boy who didn't understand the language.

"They will send me to prison. I'm a special case. I am not leaving here."

Père waited and then said, "Then I propose that you enter the novitiate of my order at Ayers Cliff, where you can consider the priesthood. I can make that happen, and they will not find you there if we are intelligent about it. We have talked about your priestly vocation before, Alfred. Your father's strength and your mother's mind. You would do well as a priest. If you spend time there and then decide you do not like the idea, you can leave when the war is over."

Mondou shook his head with a smile this time, as if to pretend that Père was simply joking, but he knew he was not. He suspected that he might stay well hidden at the novitiate. Had Père avoided the Great War the same way?

But he did not want to even pretend about it. There was nothing about the life of a priest that could ever appeal to him. He knew that Beaubien was all about two things: propagation of the faith, and procreation of the species.

Mondou preferred Père's procreation plan.

"Yes, well, we'll talk about the seminary again when we have more time," the priest said, no doubt reading Mondou's mind. "But you must understand that your life in hiding will not be easy. They are after you more than the others. I can do something for you for a while but not forever. First, it's important that you know there are others like you who are hiding out. You have friends. Actually, you're a bit of a hero among them," Père Beaubien chuckled. "So, be strong. The Lord will protect you. He wants you to be strong.

"My Christmas Midnight Mass tomorrow is at the Fieldville church. Can you get there early so that you can visit your mother's grave and we can talk more?"

Mondou thought that another trip from Lac Ste. Marie to Fieldville would be no easy task, but he nodded.

The next evening, Beaubien saw Mondou praying at his mother's grave. Beaubien walked over, knelt down, crossed himself, and said a brief prayer, then they walked back to the priest's house together.

"I prepared a Christmas present for you," the priest said.

At the house, Beaubien had clothes spread out on his bed beside a black carrying bag. There was a priest's cassock, black shoes, four collarless white shirts with four Roman clerical collars, black pants, and underwear.

Mondou smiled. At least Beaubien would have him looking like a priest.

"With your height, they will fit well. Your black overcoat is a fine match."

He gave Mondou keys to the priest's house in Farrellton, and another in Maniwaki. He also handed him some money and instructions on how and when he should feel free to use the houses. It would be either when Père knew no one would be there, or when Père himself would be the only visitor. He told Mondou that his part-time housekeepers in each place would be informed that there was a visiting priest in the vicinity who would be staying occasionally, which was not unusual. Father Foley and he shared the Gatineau houses, but Foley worked most often from his home in Martindale, and he could be managed. Other priests from the English or French diocese offices would be avoided at all costs.

"That is why we cannot make this a permanent arrangement," Beaubien warned. "Maybe for the balance of the winter. Rumours will start about the priest who never does anything priestly. There is nothing the parishioners gossip about more than their priests."

That night, Mondou was hypocrite enough to sit in his priestly robes on the shadowed side of the candle-lit altar behind the pulpit, enjoying the marvellous Christmas Mass.

It felt good to be in the church again . . . the smell of the incense; the arches and stained windows; the candles; the familiar dry taste of the host; the nostalgic sounds of old prayers and hymns.

At the beginning of his sermon, Beaubien had introduced the big, bearded priest as visiting Père Cyrois. After that, Mondou just sat, inconspicuous, scanning the church. He saw many faces he knew, including his brother and sisters. Marc's wife sat next to his brother with a small boy who was standing on the pew beside her.

Mondou spent Christmas night in the Farrellton priest's house. His reunion with his family had been difficult, and there was still a lot of catching up to do, but they had been sworn to secrecy before they left the church to go home to their fête. Père Beaubien had gone to his Masham church for a Christmas Day Mass.

After his family left, Mondou removed his soutane in what he thought was a priestly way, crawled into the generous bathtub, and stayed there for half an hour. He then pulled on one of Beaubien's collarless shirts to wear as pyjamas and fell into bed.

The bed was luxurious. There were advantages to being a priest.

He slept well beyond daylight. He had to get up to urinate, and came back to the bedroom to find himself staring at a vision.

A beautiful, fair woman in a white smock was staring at him—all of him. She was looking at a strange, dusky Adonis in an open white shirt with a strange cross around his neck, and she gasped. She couldn't move as she watched part of him reach out for her. The most exciting sight she had ever seen was unfolding in front of her.

Mondou pulled his shirt together. It didn't help.

"*Ma jolie*, how do you do?"

"*Mon Dieu*," she gasped.

Mondou smiled. The smile froze the woman where she stood. She knew she should turn and leave. She could not. He was big, dark of hair, eyes, and skin, with an expansive smile that seemed to pull her toward him. Mondou thought he should reach out to shake her hand but in changing hands, and losing the grip on his shirt, they were on each other.

They didn't have a chance to introduce themselves until forty minutes later, when they both lay naked and exhausted on the bed.

Marian sat up, swung her legs over the edge of the bed, grabbed her clothes and sat there with her head buried in her smock.

"You don't even know who I am," she said.

"That's true," answered Mondou.

"Well, I'm Marian O'Malley, and my mother is the cleaning lady for the priest's house but she's sick at home. She was supposed to clean two days ago, so I rushed over to do it. I'm filling in."

"Well, I'm very happy that you were filling in for your mother, Marie-Anne."

Marian laughed.

"Who are you?" she finally said, trying not to look at Mondou, who was still lying on the bed.

"Père Cyrois," he replied to her bare back.

"Père! A priest!" she screeched. "Mother Mary have mercy on me. Sinning the moment we meet is bad enough, but a priest. On Christmas Day! I'm going to hell." She turned on him. "What kind of priest would do this? Why didn't you tell me who you were?"

"You weren't at church yesterday? I was introduced to all the parishioners."

"I go to Mass at Martindale. Oh, my God, how will I confess this to Father Foley?"

"Confess it to me, Marie-Anne," Mondou said as he reached over and stroked her long, beautiful back.

She couldn't help smiling. "And what should I call you, Père?"

"Well, my close friends call me P'tit."

"Well, your close friends are wrong," Marian snorted. She couldn't believe the conversation she was having. This priest seemed to be trying to seduce her again, and it was working. She was more excited than ever. Was it because he was a priest, or the dozen other unholy reasons? She leaned back and let him put his mouth on her breast.

"Don't forgive me yet, Père P'tit. Not until we're done."

This time was a lot less frantic. It was slow and quiet like softly falling snow, like they had hanky-pankyed a hundred times before.

And at the end of the morning, Mondou agreed not to hear her confession until she came back to make his bed the next day.

NINE

August 1947

IN SPITE OF MAC'S reputation for laziness, just "getting by" alone on a forty-acre farm was work enough. Even if you didn't count the time he spent reading about crimes and solving them; writing and drawing; practising his harmonica; and smoking and thinking, there was lots to do.

It was hard work just staying warm all winter. Mac once told me that in the winter it got so damned cold upstairs that a glass of water would freeze solid during the night. So he slept on the ground floor with his feet almost touching the big block stove, despite the three small bedrooms on the second floor.

Gertie said Mac slept downstairs because he liked to be close to his gun and his porch, and anyone or anything that might be snooping around the yard or outbuildings. I once heard Mac tell Proulx that at night with the snow up over the windows and the lamps out to save coal oil, the farmhouse closed around him like a coffin. He couldn't sleep so he lit the lamps and prowled around, reading books and writing and drawing.

Winters went on forever in the Gatineau, and Mac had to work half the year to have enough wood to stay warm all winter. In the fall he'd go up to his grove behind the graveyard, look for a mix of dead trees and sort out the kind of wood he'd need to last the winter. He needed kindling, dry elm and ash and some maple and oak that would burn through a long winter's night, and leave a few coals so he could start the fire again in the morning.

Then the real work would begin. He'd head up the hill with a bucksaw, cut down the trees, saw them into four-foot sections, and trim off the branches with an axe. After the cutting came the hauling: down the hill and into the gulley in back of the woodshed, sometimes through the new winter snow. Once Mac had enough wood behind the shed, he'd set up a sawhorse and cut the wood into foot-and-a-half lengths for splitting. It split a lot easier if it was frozen. After the splitting, the wood had to be piled into the woodshed and then fetched all winter. As Mac would always say to me, "The wood don't get into the stove by itself, Raymond."

In winter, Mac was a hermit, but not by choice. Occasionally, when we went up from Ottawa in the winter and saw the snow blown up to the eaves of the farmhouse, we marvelled that Old Mac could live there alone at all. We'd dig our way inside, and there was the big anvil with the short axe sitting between the cot and the stove in front of the woodbox. Mac brought the anvil in from the shop to use as his chopping block. That way he hardly had to get out of bed to get his fire going in winter.

It took him half a day to dig out to the road after a winter storm, and then he'd have to hitch a ride to town with a team or a truck to get supplies, because he kept his old jalopy in the barn all winter.

If Mac were as lazy as everyone said, he would have been long dead. He had to do everything alone. Maybe being cooped up and alone all winter was why he was always on the move in the summer.

We were headed down to a Saturday night at The Coffee Shop in Mac's car. Even to a kid from downtown Ottawa, the diner was the centre of the universe. It was built facing the fork of the two main roads of Low. Across the road, on the river side, was The Paugan Inn, which featured rooms and cabins, a fancy dining room, and a bar-dance hall. Beside the Paugan parking lot were the gates to the great Paugan Dam and the Quebec Hydro properties.

The Coffee Shop was much more than a coffee shop. The interior was divided into an auto service area and a diner complete with soda bar, serving tables, pinball machines, and jukeboxes. The exterior triangular lot had gasoline pumps, benches, and large wooden lounge chairs.

Half the town of Low—and many from the surrounding towns—would gather on nights to watch what was going on in Low, at the Paugan and in and around The Coffee Shop. Many of the older folks would start on The Coffee Shop side of the street and then amble over to the Paugan bar as soon as the mood took them.

Ottawa couldn't put all that in fifty square yards.

Mac and I jumped into his jalopy and drove down to Low. Often when Mac drove to town past Miron's Point, my cousin Billy and the Miron boys would hear him coming, hide in the bush, and throw a big rock at the side of his car. Then Mac would stop the car, get out, and circle back and forth and around, cursing and trying to find the latest damage to his car.

He knew the Mirons and Billy did it, and when I asked him why he allowed them to bang up his car, he answered, "Well, they don't have much fun in these parts when they're not working, Raymond." He never drove over twenty-five miles an hour, but when he rounded Miron's Point he'd slow to fifteen so they wouldn't miss. He called it his speed bump.

They weren't throwing rocks this night. When we got to Low, The Coffee Shop was jumping, and you could hear "Baby Face" playing on the jukebox.

Mac jumped out and handed me some quarters.

"Here's some coins for the pinball, Raymond," he said. Then he walked over to Marvin Kealey, who worked as an undertaker in Wakefield, and started trouble.

"Let's talk about corpses, Marvin," Mac blurted.

One of the QPP cops was standing nearby talking to Billy in a friendly way, even though Billy had just stolen his police car the week before when I was in The Coffee Shop playing pinball. The cops had been in there playing poker with the garage mechanics and they didn't even raise their heads from their card game when they heard the police siren wailing away.

"Ain't that your car?" someone said to the cops.

"Yeah, it's just Billy running around town again. Guess we left the keys in it."

Billy was only a few years older than me, which meant he was too young to drive.

When I told Mac about it, he chuckled for a long, long time. "Well, they know he's been driving a tractor since he could walk. Anyway, a good cop should have all the right enemies, but up here a lot of the QPP are locals and they don't want any enemies. Lord, they're related to half the people they arrest."

"What corpses?" one of the cops said. "Are you still stirring up shit about missing folks and bush zombies, Mac?"

"Are you eavesdropping on my talking?" Mac said.

"Never seen you not talking, Mac, so it's hard not to be listening."

Billy was about to saunter over to the Paugan with the bigger boys, even though he was too young to drink, but he interrupted my listening by sticking his freckles in my face.

"Where did you get to?"

I knew what he was talking about but said, "What do you mean?"

"I mean, me bucko, there's a lot of stookin' left to be done. And there's early milkin' before everyone's off to church, and I don't intend to be feeling too good in the morning. Brian is pretendin' he's too sick to work. That leaves you. So bring your dumb dog and your sorry arse on home tonight so you'll be ready to help with the chores early. You hear me? Come in home tonight."

Then Billy sauntered across to the inn.

You didn't cross Billy. He was full of piss and vinegar.

I told Mac I had to go to Cals' that night, so we decided to drive home. On the way, Mac told me that after talking to Connor, the gravedigger, and Marvin from the funeral home, he was developing a theory about our zombie on the hill. Marvin told him there was a body in the Mondou grave, and Connor told Mac that Mondou was buried when Mac was down in Wakefield with his goitre problem a few Decembers back.

Connor said, "Mac, they always wait until spring, but this time they wanted him buried right then and there after the funeral. The December ground is as hard as Gatineau granite, which is a billion years hard, and I told them I'd be digging for a week to carve out a cavity deep enough for the coffin. But you know what Beaubien said? He said he likes the flow of the service from the church across the road to the graveside. He said it was good for them who was grieving. But there was practically no one there grieving at the funeral, from what I could see. Anyway, they agreed that I could get other men and pickaxes and enter the ground far enough to bury a thin box, and they'd pay extra. Foley didn't say a word, and he's cheaper than Judas. So we did it."

Mac was quiet for a while, focusing on his driving.

"Strange that Foley would be so involved in a funeral from Fieldville. He's got enough of his own Irish to be burying. Why didn't they bury Mondou in Fieldville beside his father and mother? Also strange that again I was told to mind my own business. Marvin said that the zombies had enough trouble with the army, RCMP informers, bounty hunters, and the QPP. He told me to stay out of it. Anyway, Alfred Mondou is now dead as a doornail as far as everybody in Ottawa is concerned, but as Dickens said, 'There are things deader than doornails.'"

I was so confused. Zombies were the living dead and not as dead as doornails or anything else.

Mac had pulled up to the farmhouse but didn't get out of the car right away. He just kept talking like he was figuring things out.

"Did you ever know something but pretend to yourself that you didn't know it because nobody wants you to know it, and knowing it would make everything so damned difficult?"

He stopped, but I knew he didn't really expect me to answer. I could hear Smoky barking and howling from the house because he'd heard the jalopy, and he missed us so.

I jumped out of the jalopy, shouting, "Okey dokey, Smoky."

I let him out to leap all over me and pee, and leap all over Mac and pee and sniff. It was so dark, and he was so black, you couldn't see Smoky half the time.

Mac was still mumbling away, and then he asked me a question.

"Do you know about Robin Hood?"

"Everybody knows about Robin Hood."

"Well, with everything I've been hearing, I don't think we have the Scarlet Pimpernel. We have Robin Hood. And his merry men. And two Friar Tucks."

Suddenly Mac let out a yelp that was louder than Smoky's.

"Mother of God! It's been as plain as the nose on my face."

Nothing could be as plain as the nose on Mac's face except maybe his goitre.

"His right-hand man. The graveyard. The brains."

Right-hand brains man in the graveyard.

Smoky was leaping all over us, and I kept saying, "Wanna go for a walk, wanna go for a walk?"

It drove Smoky even crazier, so I told Mac I'd head out to Cals' so I'd be ready to work in the morning.

TEN

January 1945

MONDOU AGREED with Beaubien that he should meet with a small group of zombies in Maniwaki. He wanted to know about their status. Were the Feds still searching for them? When did they expect to come out of hiding? Did they expect a pardon eventually? How did they live? How did they earn a living?

He didn't want friends or allies. He didn't trust anyone, but if he were going to help himself and his family, he needed to know more. Beaubien gave him a train ticket from Farrellton to Maniwaki, and he went dressed as Père Cyrois.

That night in the priest's house in Maniwaki, he met two Frenchmen, two Algonquin from the reservation, and a small, wild-looking Irishman who introduced himself as "Murph." The Irishman had already told Père Beaubien that there were other Irish zombies living in the woods west of Venosta.

"They live in a small cabin, hunt wild game for their food, and they're ill-fed creatures, that's for sure. They have a miserable existence. There's a lot of misery out there. You see these two, Priest?"

Mondou nodded.

"Ox and Snow Man. Two better men you'll never meet. They're Algonquin. They used to own Canada. Now they don't own land or the homes they live in. They're not even allowed to vote, but Ottawa wants them to go and die in Germany. And me? I'd rather bomb Belfast than Berlin. Ireland stayed neutral in this war, you know. After what the Brits done to the Irish, my cousins over there won't go to their war, and they don't want us going to no Brit war, either. There's a lot of us that won't go to their war. We're in good company. The rich won't go. The unnneeeversityyy crowd won't go."

Then Murph did a little jig leap while pointing at Mondou and said, "The fuckin' priests won't go. The firemen won't go. The cops won't go. None of them go—the RCMP, the QPP, the Ottawa cops. Fuck, even prisoners don't go. And the politicians won't go. Jesus Murphy, they were so scared of losing their jobs they didn't even vote to make zombies go until a month ago; five years later, with the war almost over and nearly 50,000 dead. We knew they'd break their promise. That's why we stayed away from all their bullshit."

Murph turned to get a big grin of approval from his native friends, and Mondou noticed that the two Frenchmen were smiling, too. "I know friends and relatives of politicians who knew they'd never get called up to go. The bureaucrats don't go. Relatives of bureaucrats don't go. We're in the best of company, Priest. I can even give you names of guys who sweep the goddamned rail lines that don't go. Exemptions for essential services, my ass. And those folks don't have to hide in the bush. We do. There are lots of us in the bush."

Mondou was concluding that Murph was one of the fastest talkers he'd ever heard, and that his language did not improve in the presence of clergy. "So on this side of the Gatineau there's the Venosta group, a sadder bunch of arseholes I never did see. Then there's a group down near Wakefield who run back and forth as far as Wolf Lake. They live in a cave through the winter. And I hear there's another group hiding in Lafleche Caverns. It's a long winter, but Jesus Murphy, if you ask me, Wakefield's too damned close to army headquarters and the Parliament in Ottawa."

Mondou wasn't going to ask why Murph felt that an army that worked its way from the Pacific to the Atlantic and over to Europe would struggle much with the extra sixty-mile run up to Maniwaki but he said nothing. Murph was still spinning, and Mondou was starting to hear a low hum that began to sound rhythmical. Murph noticed the confusion on Mondou's face as he looked around the room. "Pay no attention to that. Ox starts to chant when I'm in a rant. He'll get louder the longer I go, but it won't stop me. You listen, Priest. Just listen. It's important you know this, and nobody in Canada knows more about it than me."

Mondou was staring at Ox. He could tell the sound was coming from Ox but could just see a smile. Two low notes, drumming over and over, rising like water from the floor, "Hey YaNa NaNa NaNa, Hey YaNa NaNa NaNa . . ." but the background noise was not bothering Murph.

"Quebec is full of folks like us. There's a mountain near Chicoutimi where there's over a hundred hiding. They call them 'absentees.' I don't know much about them except there was a riot when the RCMP and military police went looking up there. And they're hiding in the rest of Canada, too. Jesus Murphy, the chief, Ox's father, told us about a bunch of immigrant Italians hiding by a reservation up near the Lake Superior end of the St. Mary's River. Everyone in Sault Ste. Marie knows about them. They call them the 'Crazy Cap Commandos,' or something. They must be crazy. They're afraid of being deported to Italy to fight for Mussolini. Can you believe that? Mackenzie will get them in the king's army before Italy does. Everyone knows they're there, but the RCMP won't find them because as long as they've got a job looking, they won't be going to war themselves. It's all a shitty business. I could tell you about them hiding down East if the chief would stop his wailing. One guy escaped from a train in New Brunswick, and we've even got our local zombieman, Mondou, who escaped from a train right near Montreal."

Mondou interrupted quickly. "How do you know all this?"

"I study it. I read everything about it. Nothing else to do. A story appears and then suddenly disappears, so I cut them out of the paper and keep them. They bury the mutiny stories from the camps across Canada. They've been happening all the way to the coast. I got a B.C. mutiny story from *Le Droit*. The French paper. I can't speak it but I can read it."

Suddenly, Murph stopped his rant. He stared at Mondou. Mondou didn't like it. The long silence suddenly stopped the chant emanating from Ox.

Then Murph continued in a slower, different, quiet tone. "The Algonquin get a lot of news from other reservations right across the country. The local cops even like to tell stories they pick up from inside their system but I don't want to talk about that. They're friends of mine and maybe yours." Murph paused again, staring even more intently at Mondou.

Mondou had a need to fill the silence so he asked, "Are these people all zombies?"

"I told you. Some are called 'absentees.' Some draft dodgers that the army and NRMA never got in the first place, like me, and Ox, and Snow Man and those two, Gilles and Paul. Some are deserters from the regular army. Some are zombies who escaped because they felt like they were prisoners in the camps, and they knew King would break his promise anyway. Myself, I like working alone except for my dodger friend, Ox here."

Murph nodded toward Ox, and Mondou did the same, and Ox nodded back. Murph pulled a chair very close and finally sat down and leaned to face Mondou and said quietly, "It has been a long war, Père. Five fucking years already. We've even had Americans that dropped by the reservation after their country joined the war a couple of years ago. They said they were conscientious objectors. I said, 'We locked up our Jehovah's witnesses before you Americans even got into the war. Your chances here are slim and none. And you won't like the weather; so why don't you head south where it's a lot warmer.'

We didn't want their goddamned American cops up here nosing around. We got our own problems. Now, let me tell you about the riots that are starting in the zombie camps and the marches across the country—"

The chanting started again and very loud this time. Suddenly, Ox rose to his feet and walked toward the two Frenchmen. Over his shoulder he said, "Enough, Irish. The Irish can talk forever, Père. We have to go." In French, Ox said a few words quietly to the two men, and Mondou heard Père Beaubien mentioned. The three shook hands while Murph kept talking at Mondou. Mondou heard one of the men say, "*Bonne chance, Chef,*" while looking over at Murph and shaking his head. They opened the door, waved at the priest, and walked out.

Ox turned and said, "Enough, Murph. The rest is all the same." Ox came over and stood directly behind Murph. Mondou could see that Ox was twice as big as Murph, but Murph didn't move. He kept staring at Mondou. "Ox is the boss, Mondou. You see, Ox is not his real name. His real name is Oxawatic. That means he's a direct descendant of the KEE:Ontwogky who was a great Algonquin chief back in the early eighteenth century. Well, I thought I heard an Ox in there somewhere, and he's as big as one, so I started to call him Ox Blood. He likes the name all right."

Ox said, "Do I have to carry you out of here, Irish?" but Murph kept right on talking. "So Ox and I can move on and off the reservation, sometimes into Maniwaki when it suits us, and into the bush some nights when the heat is on. I couldn't live like those miseries near Venosta. You ever eaten squirrel, Priest? Well, you don't want to."

Ox was nodding in agreement. He even made the room look small. It would take more than squirrels to fuel that furnace. Ox was now grabbing the shoulders of Murph's coat. "We go. This is not the confessional. The priest knows enough."

"This priest won't say a thing about tonight—right, Père?" Murph was staring hard. "So now I ask you: What's a nice priest like you doing, sticking your holy nose into our business?"

"Well, maybe the church can help you," Mondou blurted.

Murph suddenly let out such a screech both Mondou and Ox were startled. "*You'll* be needing the help, Priest!" With that, Murph leaped to his feet, knocking over his chair, and shouted, "Jesus Murphy, Ox, I know who this priest is. I know who's behind that bullshit beard. You're French, and a friend of Beaubien and I've seen your picture. This priest ain't going to be talking about this meeting to anyone, Ox. He's a wanted man. It's Mondou. Alfred P'tit Mondou, that's who!"

Then, for some reason, Ox, after bending and staring into Mondou's face, gathered a big grin, and raised his hands toward the ceiling as Murph jigged around the room.

Mondou shouted, "Be smart! You, too, are wanted by the army. More than ever."

"Ahhh . . . but not like you, Mondou. You, my friend, are a cop killer, a mutineer, a revolutionary. You're big time. I'm surprised Beaubien ever let you out of his sight. Maybe he doesn't know how badly they're beating the bushes trying to find you. Or maybe the army doesn't trust Beaubien. You better hope those Frenchies didn't recognize you. They want you so bad, they'd give all of us a pass if we turned you in."

As Murph talked, he was now weaving around Mondou in a slow ballet, and Mondou was thinking: *more treachery*. Meeting other zombies had been a mistake. While sitting in lock-up in Terrace, he had made a vow to be a lone wolf. He had broken that vow and was already facing the consequences.

Ox then stopped staring at the ceiling, made a slight move of his head toward Murph, who broke out into a big grin and was back to a short two-step.

"No, Monsieur Mondou, you can relax. The last person in the Gatineau to ever turn on someone would be yours truly. Ask anybody. Eh, Ox?"

Mondou didn't expect to get anything but a nod from Ox, and that's what he got.

"Now, let us give you some advice. First, you'd better hope that those two frogs didn't recognize you. It didn't look like it. I was watching them. Maybe they did recognize you but because you're a pea soup, they won't tell anyone. I love that priest getup."

Murph went on to suggest that dressed as priest or no priest, the train was not the way to travel. The authorities watched the train most carefully.

"They know that without a car or registration, or a licence to drive, the train is your only alternative. There's a ticket master at every station and they all have photos, and you're one of them. I've seen your photo a few times. It's in the Maniwaki station now."

Murph said it was best to pick an area and stay put. He admitted that he had befriended Ox because of his access to the reservation. Ox just nodded quietly. Mondou found himself wondering what Ox got out of the relationship. Probably someone who could talk them out of any trouble they encountered off the reservation.

"We always have a full stomach, and that's a lot better than crawling around looking for small game in the bush, especially in the winter. I can't stand that shit. I'd rather have the food in an army jail." Ox just nodded. Food certainly seemed to be a priority issue, and Mondou, remembering the interminable Gatineau winter, could understand why. He himself couldn't eat free on the Lord for much longer.

Mondou began to relax about the Irishman with the mile-a-minute mouth. He did not intend to stay in one place, and needing to be in constant hiding would be the same as prison. It certainly would not be freedom. But it also started to occur to him that he needed help—more help than Beaubien could provide.

As Murph was preparing to leave, Mondou asked, "So how should I get back down the Gatineau to Lac Ste. Marie or Farrellton?"

Murph smiled. "You've learned already why we stay put. It's the worst part, just getting around."

"You're saying I can't leave Maniwaki?"

"I'm saying it's a long walk." Murph looked over at Ox for a few seconds, then turned back to Mondou. "Look, I'll give you a phone number that will reach me at the reserve. When you're ready to go, Ox can use a rig that belongs to the band for a day, and he has a band licence. We'll get you down the line but it's not something we can do twice. As I told you, this life is not convenient."

"Why would you two do that? Why take the chance?"

Murph paused and then repeated his hysterical laugh. "Because, my man, you're big-time. A bigwig. The Frenchmen call you *ZombieGars*. ZombieMan. You're famous, Mondou. I've got your clippings. There's an Ottawa army guy who's even getting press because he's declared he wants to see you hang. This Grafftey guy is promising amnesty to any zombie or absentee who turns you in."

Mondou felt a shiver when he heard the name Grafftey. The corporal who harassed him in Petawawa. Probably the same one who raided the family farm.

"So you see, Mondou, Ox and I are just goddamned proud to know you, and we sure don't want to see those miserable bastards catch big game." Ox nodded again. Then Murph stood, did a little silent jig, and said good night. Ox trailed out behind him.

Mondou spent another day and a half at the Maniwaki priest house making plans and made a few phone calls under the name of Père Cyrois. He would need one more big favour from Beaubien, which he called to arrange, and a big favour from his new fans, Ox and Murph.

"Murph, it's me, Père Cyrois."

"I haven't talked to a priest twice in one week since I was an altar boy. How are you doing, good Father?"

"Well, I need you and Ox and the band truck, but it will be a two-way trip. Down to Low and then back up to the reserve garage with a load. Can you arrange that?"

"Well, if we're going down, we have to come back the same day, so I guess so. But then you'll still be up here, P'tit."

"The next time we have to go anywhere I'll drive you, Murph. And please don't call me P'tit or Mondou. Let's use Père for now."

"How did you know about the band's garage?"

"Priests know everything."

Ox and Murph picked him up the next morning. They didn't ask any questions about the purpose of their trip. Murph seemed excited that he was on a mission with the infamous ZombieMan. When he wasn't talking he sang while strumming on a tiny guitar that he called his Irish. Mondou liked the sound coming out of the little man and said so. "It sounds like it's coming from far away."

Murph stared at Mondou. "It's coming from across the sea, Mondou. My grandfather was a harper with an instrument on his knee half as big as he was. Jesus Murphy, he could sing."

Mondou laughed. "You say Jesus Murphy the way other English in the army say 'fuck.'"

"Me fadder was a drunk. My name was Jesus, my brother was Christ. Every time me father said Jesus Christ, we knew he'd be hitting both of us." Murph strummed and sang again, "Jesus loves me, this I know, cuz the Bible tells me so . . ."

Mondou listened and thought about his two new friends. He knew that if Murph and Ox didn't completely trust him now, they would be happier with the relationship in a few weeks.

ELEVEN

August 1947

I PICKED UP SMOKY and headed for the Cals' place along the road because it was too dark to go across the fields and through the bush. Anyway, all the talk was making me nervous. Everything seemed to be about graves and gravestones, zombies and coffins. Mac obviously believed in zombies and never stopped talking about them.

My great-aunt Gertie believed in ghosts and had been talking about them for years. Earlier that summer, even my mom saw the Gertie ghost she'd been hearing about for so long. She and Gertie had been sitting on the front porch and heard some movement inside, and then turned to see a woman standing and staring at the parlour where so many family members had been waked. It was Gertie's aunt, the same woman whose picture hung over the bed in the front bedroom.

While I was walking and thinking the worst possible thoughts, I reached the lowest part of the road where the creek ran under it. It was the creek that separated Mac's property from the Cals'. It was overcast and so dark that I could hear the trickle of the creek but couldn't see it. I could barely see Smoky scampering a few feet in front of me. It was as dark as the inside of a cow.

Suddenly, two men just appeared out of the bush. They were walking toward me.

Smoky sank to his haunches, making his long, low growl. I'd never seen anybody walking that road at night, and with all the talk about zombies, I started to quake before I knew I was scared.

The two men stopped right in front of me. They looked like Mutt and Jeff from the comics. One was very big with an upside-down mouth and a big hat pulled over his eyes, and the other was a little guy with crazy red hair, and he made me think of a leprechaun.

The elf was talking, but I couldn't understand him at first because his tongue was thick with liquor, and when he leaned into my face, I smelled it.

The big man bent over and put the back of his hand toward Smoky in a friendly way, and Smoky snuck forward to smell him.

All at once, the man snapped out and caught Smoky by the throat, and with his hand tangled in Smoky's collar he lifted him above his head with only one arm. Smoky was wriggling, and struggling and choking.

They were zombies, all right.

I ran toward the big zombie but the little one grabbed me by the shoulders and put his face in mine and said, "We were on our way to murder Old Mac. And the next time, we'll kill him, you, and your dog, too. You tell him to forget all this snooping around about zombies. It's none of his business and it's none of your business."

It seemed like a long time, because Smoky was now hanging there limp, coughing and whimpering, but when he finished talking, the little zombie waved his hand at the big zombie. Then the big zombie dropped Smoky onto the gravel, and Smoky limped to the side of the road and crawled into the bushes.

"You deliver our message to Old Mac now, you hear? And don't talk to the QPP or anyone else about this. It will go an awful lot worse for you, hear?"

Then they both turned and walked back the way they came,

and I ran over to find Smoky. I sat in the ditch hugging him until we both stopped trembling. He kept hacking. There was something wrong with his throat.

I tried to pick him up, but no matter how I grabbed him it seemed that I was hurting his throat. I took off my jacket and worked it underneath him, and started to pull him through the long grass along the side of the gravel road. I backed up, lurching, and he rolled off the coat.

I finally sat beside him in the dark and stroked his head. I wanted Smoky to talk so bad so he could tell me what to do.

I was never so sad as I was sitting on the side of that road with my sick Smoky.

After a while, Smoky struggled to his feet, and stumbled a bit and then started to creep along the side of the road toward Mac's. He knew where I wanted him to go. I cried, and Smoky coughed all the way home, but we made it.

I told Mac everything while he was looking at Smoky's throat and trying to make him swallow some water. Smoky was getting worse, maybe from the walk. Mac wrapped him with the blanket from the top of his bed and carried him out and put him in the rumble seat of the jalopy.

"Don't you be worryin' none, Raymond. We'll get Smoky out to Martin and he'll fix him up. He's better than any doctor with the animals."

I was still babbling while we drove along Cal Road. I knew it was because I was so frightened about Smoky that I couldn't stop talking.

"The little red-headed zombie said it was none of our business, Mac. That's what he said. So I don't know what you've been trying to find out but let's not know it. These zombies aren't like Robin Hood, Mac. They're killers."

Mac kept driving while staring intently at the road, like it was going to disappear around the next corner.

He started talking to himself but they weren't fun ditties this time.

"Who did this? Who knew? O'Sullivan. Foley. The Coffee Shop crowd? Someone got this bunch after us tonight."

I yelled at Mac.

"Mac! Brian and Billy and lots of others don't know this truth you're after. Why do you have to know it?" I could hear myself getting madder and madder, so he didn't say another word.

We pulled into Uncle Martin's, but by the time he looked at Smoky, there was blood on the rumble seat and Smoky was dead. While Mac was telling Uncle Martin that Smoky's collar got caught in a fence running from a coyote, Aunt Mabel couldn't calm me down. I remember us arguing about taking me back to the city the next morning, but I had a fit. I shouted that I was going to bury Smoky on the hill in the cemetery before I went home. I screamed about staying with Smoky.

Finally, Uncle Martin said, "Let the boy bury his dog."

TWELVE

February 1945

OX AND MURPH had never seen a man work as smart and as fast as Mondou.

They had the snow tractor up and running after working on it for two weeks in the reserve garage.

It was an incredible thing. It was "souped up," as Mondou said, and in the snow it could run three times faster than the fastest horses and sleigh. They rearranged the interior to change it from a seven-passenger to four-passenger, expanding the cargo area to allow for supplies, guns and ammunition, and what Mondou called "contraband." They also added a small heater. Mondou assumed that they'd be spending some nights sleeping in the tractor.

Murph wondered whether they should have space for a bigger gang.

"We need speed," Mondou said. "As it is, we'll have one more space than we'll ever need. We're going to remain a small wolf pack."

Mondou told them that the tractor had been built in Valcourt by a man called Armand Bombardier. They tried one at the Paugan before the war, but it kept breaking down because they were poor at maintaining machines. They went back to teams of horses to haul equipment across the dam, he said, which was stupid and dangerous. He did not sound happy about folks at the Hydro.

When Mondou called Valcourt to try to buy a snow tractor, Bombardier said that the Canadian government had issued wartime rationing regulations. He would have to prove that snowmobiles were essential to his livelihood in order to buy one.

Mondou smiled, "I could have said that I was a priest who had to chase through snow to save sinners, or a criminal having to escape the police. Instead I asked about the old machine at the Paugan. They said as far as they knew, it was still there." To keep their business going, Bombardier had to switch to developing vehicles for the military. There were probably less than a dozen snow tractors in operation in the province, and those were being used to collect maple syrup in the woods of southeastern Quebec.

"If I could get the ski tractor owned by Hydro, we'd be the only ones in the Gatineau with a machine."

He didn't bother to tell Ox and Murph that Beaubien had contacted Hydro for him, and then drove into the Paugan and found the ski tractor abandoned behind the Hydro sheds, and had someone make arrangements to pay a token price for it as scrap.

Murph and Ox did not think the pile of junk was worth hauling up to Maniwaki but were resigned to the fact that it would be the last favour they would do for this Frenchman.

They would quickly change their minds.

A couple of weeks later, Murph and Ox brought up the subject of a camp. They did not want to live too far from the reservation and friends, and they had the perfect place now that they didn't have to hike in. It even had a cave they could use on the worst winter days.

Mondou liked the cave idea, but he wanted to make sure the location was remote enough. Ox and Murph assembled supplies and packed them in the tractor while Mondou prepared his machine for the more rigorous test run. He protested when he saw a roll of canvas that took up half the supply space, but Murph and Ox said they needed it to cover the mouth of the cave.

They headed out to Petit Lac du Cerf with a full load and one extra passenger, the Algonquin called Snow. Mondou had come to trust Snow while working in the garage. Mondou was constantly talking about the cabin they would build beside the cave if he liked the site. Ox kept telling Mondou that Snow was a great "builder of cabins," and Snow, Ox, and Murph would laugh at some shared joke.

Petit Lac du Cerf was south and east of the reserve and far east of the main highway into Maniwaki, where there were no passable winter trails. By the time they reached the site, Mondou knew that only one machine could ever access the location in winter, and they owned it. He also loved the camp location, back on a plateau overlooking the cave and lake.

The location allowed them an escape south and east if his pursuers ever appeared in the vicinity of Maniwaki. There were no roads beyond the east side of the endlessly long Thirty One Mile Lake, and more water than land leading right up to the Baskatong Reservoir. They could head out in a hundred directions. The only folk Ox had ever come across out here were from the Gatineau Fish and Game Club at the very south end of the lake.

Ox and Murph had watched as Mondou kept testing then adapting the snow machine through fifteen-hour days. He added more support and strong steel bars that ran along the bottom of the skis. He soldered carrier hooks onto the back and sides of the cabin. He was always adding power and improving the ignition. He said he never wanted a stall at a critical time. He told them anxiously that he wanted to return and make improvements on the tractor. His instinct said he had to move fast.

"We've been in one place too long and we'll never get another garage where the tractor work can be done. I want it to be perfect."

"Go make it perfect, Mondou. You know the route. Follow your trail. The weather is fine. The three of us will start setting up camp. You come back in three days," Murph said. Ox nodded.

"I've got plans for the cabin I want to build," Mondou answered.

"You got your goddamned plans for everything, Mondou. Now we're tired of your orders. The tractor's unloaded. You head back. Three days."

Three days later, after working almost without sleep, Mondou was back at the site, gloriously happy with his tank.

But when he looked at his camp, he gasped, "What the fuck is that?"

Ox, Snow, and Murph were too drunk to give him much of an answer.

"We're celebrating the completion of our new cabin, Mondou," Murph said, and all three of them sat below the camp on the plateau, and howled with laughter.

Mondou watched with great interest as Ox and Snow locked down the teepee and slid it into the cave so that it would be in good shape when they returned. Then the three of them packed up what Mondou was now calling the SkiTank. All the while, Murph carefully carved a message on the cave wall near the entrance: *Abandon hope, ye who enter here.*

On a fine winter morning, they all headed back toward Maniwaki and the reservation, feeling content about their new home. Ox and Snow explained how they had stripped and hauled seventeen long, slim poles of spruce and pine out of the bush and assembled them, creating a large circle on the ground. They then prepared the final pole with the canvas attached, locating the door where the two ends of canvas came together. The teepee was twenty-two feet across, with a firepit in the centre, and it slept the four of them comfortably.

Most important, they had built it in a day. Mondou was beginning to realize they might have to do it many times.

Mondou was in love with his new home, but Snow had to return to his family. Mondou had also had a call from Père Beaubien at the garage telling him that officials around Low and Fieldville were asking questions again. It was only a matter of time before someone started to notice something about all his endeavours in the Maniwaki area. He was reconciled to a life on the run. Before he left the reservation, Mondou restocked the tractor and threw in Murph's Irish, his single action .22, and Ox's pride and joy, a pump-action, seven-shot .22 Winchester.

He soon found out that he'd been clairvoyant. As they neared the back approach to the reservation, Snow ordered him to stop.

"See dose red lights through the trees? That's not right. Stay here." They sat in the dark for a half hour before Snow trudged back. "Get yourselves outta here, boys. Dis time it's the army and the RCMP and they're not leavin' without you, Mondou."

They headed south, following the railway bed. It was just past dusk, and well after the train had already made its run back from Maniwaki to Ottawa. Mondou was thinking it might be time to set up a second camp in the hills above Lac Ste. Marie behind Baldface Mountain, fifty miles away.

Murph sat behind Ox, strumming on his Irish and singing drinking songs. Murph was sending Mondou a message. Mondou hadn't packed whiskey. Mondou wasn't much of a drinker, but he understood them. Most of his family drank too much, including his father and brother. Murph and Ox were always looking for an excuse to celebrate just about anything, including sunset. Throughout the evening on the way south, with the moon beginning to reflect through the clouds, Murph kept insisting that he and Ox deserved to stop and pick up a bottle in Kazabazua, at the Longest Bar in the Gatineau. After all, it was right on the rail line.

"There'll be no harm done. No Mounties left to bother us if

they're all in Maniwaki. And dere not after us, dere after you," Murph argued.

"There's still the QPP, and I'm not stopping. So shut up."

Murph kept whining with his mile-a-minute mouth as they passed behind Farley and Bouchette and went through Grace-field. After more than two hours of moaning, he was getting more miserable as they approached Kazabazua.

Mondou knew drunks, and knew that unless Murph and Ox got a drink, the whining would never end.

He agreed to stop so they could get in and get out of the bar with their bottle. He knew the area around the Longest Bar in the Gatineau well.

"I'll stay in hiding across the road by the tracks behind the church. You should be back before I finish a cigarette."

Mondou could hear the jukebox from the bar playing "Let It Snow," which he found strange, since there was enough snow in the Gatineau to cover all of Quebec.

He hadn't even finished his cigarette before he heard shouting, and seconds later Murph came staggering out of the bar and started running toward Mondou.

"They're killing Ox," he yelled.

"How the fuck could this happen so fast?" Mondou asked. Murph slipped on the road and fell forward, and Mondou could see that the top of his head was bleeding. He'd probably been hit with a beer bottle.

From his knees Murph shouted, "They're killing him. Bring my gun."

Mondou reached into the tractor and pulled out Ox's gun. He thought of covering his priest's garb with the white Indian wool, but there was no time.

Mondou ran past Murph and entered the vestibule shed that protected the entrance. He peered through the pane on the inner door.

Just to the right, not twenty paces away, Ox was on his back. One man had his knee on Ox's chest, another seemed to be straddled across his legs, and a third was on his knees punching him from above and behind.

Ox was still fighting to get up, which was a good sign.

Mondou opened the door and walked in cool, collected and in control. He pointed his rifle over the melee and fired.

All sound stopped except the music from the jukebox, which was now playing "I'll Walk Alone." Somewhere in the back of his mind he acknowledged that if he had walked alone, none of this would be happening.

Everyone turned to look at the priest with rifle. Even Ox lay still.

"Help him get up. Ox, get out of here!" Mondou shouted with his rifle trained at the man on his knees behind Ox.

Then Mondou heard a voice from his left.

"Who the fuck are you?"

A big man in suspenders was standing at the bar, reaching for a quart beer bottle.

Mondou turned the rifle toward him. "Leave that bottle just where it is." The man looked familiar.

"You doggone bastard priest." The man had his grip on the bottle, and he came toward Mondou, who didn't know whether he was going to throw it or stagger over and pound him with it.

Mondou fired, hit the Molson's bottle right on the label, and glass flew everywhere.

The man was left holding the neck and jagged top of the bottle, and was looking up at his hand. Mondou shifted the rifle toward the three who were still on Ox, and they all backed off and away.

"Move, friend. Out of here," Mondou said, and Ox got up and started to stumble toward the door.

But the man at the bar wasn't finished. Mondou hadn't taken his eyes off of him.

It was Munro, Grafftey's son-of-a-bitch flunky.

Munro made a lunge toward Mondou with the jagged beer bottle. There was another shot. This time the rest of the bottle neck and blood flew and splattered the mirror behind the bar. The big man screamed and bent to his knees, holding his bloody hand in his crotch.

Mondou shouted over the man's wailing and the jukebox's singing.

"If one of you steps out this door to follow us, I'll put the next shot right through your nose." Then he backed out the door.

Murph had been peering in through the bar window, and he helped Mondou manoeuvre Ox across the road into the darkness behind the church. They put Ox in the back.

"Murph, get in with him and use the kit to fix yourselves up. And keep an eye on that bar door as we pull out of here." Mondou could hear the jukebox playing "Don't Fence Me In" as he started up the motor. Within moments, they were headed back to the rail line.

Back in the bar, Marian O'Malley had been laughing with Liette, her old friend from grade school in Low. The bar was always noisy but just now there were more than the usual roars coming from around the corner to her right.

"I'll get us another draft," Liette said.

"I don't want one. Tell my brother it's time to go."

Liette was already headed toward the bar. She glanced to her right, and there was the big Indian lying on the floor and laughing. She'd seen his act before.

By the time she reached the bar, the shit hit the fan. Munro's boys had jumped on the Indian and were trying to pin him down. The sound level soared.

Liette gave up on the beer and tapped Marian's brother, Seany Boy, on the ass. She mouth-whispered "Marian" and gave him a head movement toward the front door. He nodded and raised his half empty glass toward her. They both knew that if

Marian wanted to go, it was time to go. He also knew that it was his last chance with Liette. Tomorrow night he'd be back at Petawawa, and within the week he'd be on a ship bound for northwest Europe.

Liette headed back to the table. Marian had already slipped on her boots and dug her mitts out of her coat pocket. The shouting and fighting seemed to be shifting the whole saloon.

"We better sit till dere done," Liette said. "We'll never get troo the door. They're beatin' up the Indian."

Marian had a ringside seat. She watched the tall priest shoot off Munro's hand.

It was the same priest she had spent time with in Farrellton.

Marian was shaking as she watched P'tit back out of the bar with Ox.

"Marian, you're shivering," Liette said. "It's okay. The shooting is over. It's all right, now."

I'm not shaking, Marian thought. *I'm having an orgasm.*

She had to find this phony priest. And she would pursue him until he was hers.

⁂

Murph announced that no one had come out of the bar as far as he could see. Mondou assumed that the bartender was doing the obvious thing—calling the police. He approached the tracks and began to turn south.

"Go north, Mondou," Ox said.

"The army and RCMP are north, Ox."

"They arrested my father up there. The chief is in jail."

Mondou turned the snow tractor. He wasn't going to go far north. He needed time to think through the latest events. His first thought was that he would have to get rid of these two dumb drunks and go it alone.

He turned and looked over his shoulder to see Ox patching up Murph.

"Murph, Ox is doing most of the bleeding. What's going on?"

"Ox is tough as nails," Murph shouted over the sound of the motor. "He'll fix hisself up."

Then Murph reached over to grab the rifle and said, "You should have killed him with that second bullet. That was Mad Munro whose hand you shot off. He's a fucking nutcase. He was thrown out of the army because they knew he was a homicidal maniac. He tried to kill a sergeant at Camp Petawawa. He talks like he's a fucking war hero, and he never left Canada, and he and his veteran buddy hate zombies. They're bounty hunters."

Mondou's heart sank. It *had been* Munro, the very same brute who had tormented him at Petawawa.

"I'd hardly had two drags of my cigarette. They must have been waiting for you. What the hell happened in there? How'd they do it, Ox? They had you pinned on your back in seconds."

Murph answered, as usual.

"That gang had mouthed off before about us being draft dodgers. This time they shouted something about Ox joining his father in jail, and Ox starts on his back. I told you he's an Oxy Moron."

"He starts on his back?"

"He's an Indian leg wrestler. Best in the Gatineau. He makes money on his back like a prostitute. He walks in, lies down, and shouts for takers at five bucks a go. This time they just piled on."

"*Tabernac*, you two are trouble. Too much trouble."

Murph was still fiddling with the rifle.

"It's a good thing Mad Munro and the gang thought that you were holding more shots," he said, "or we'd be in bad shape by now. This gun is empty."

Mondou looked over his shoulder again at Ox. Ox had a deep, low laugh that never escaped through his mouth. It just caused him to heave and shake, like he was gasping for breath. He was starting to heave, and Murph picked it up and started bouncing up and down with his high-pitched howl.

Choking with tears, Ox grabbed the rifle from Murph and started loading it. Then he reached over and leaned it on the passenger seat beside Mondou.

"Your gun now. You're the best shooter I've ever seen. You would have been a good warrior."

Mondou was trying to ignore them both. He was now being chased by the Quebec Provincial Police, the army, the RCMP, and a gang of maniacs who wanted to catch him or kill him, and he was going in the wrong direction . . . faster and faster into each new disaster with these two. It was time for a talk.

He pulled into a grove west of the tracks a few miles north of Kaz, killed the motor, and they sat there in the dark.

"What in God's name are you sitting here for, you dumb Pepsi?"

Mondou ignored Murph.

"Ox, we can't go north. There's only one QPP car to the south. We can circle behind him and make it across Lac Ste. Marie to a cottage I know. After tonight, we might have to go a lot farther."

"God sent us into that bar, Mondou," Ox said. "The man you shot shouted down into my face. They locked up my father and they're taking him to Ottawa. Those bounty bums said they were making a citizen's arrest and grabbed me. I would never have known they had taken my father. Why would the army arrest an old man?"

"Because they want me, Ox," Mondou groaned. "You two and your tribe will do better without me."

Ox closed his eyes. "If they get him to Ottawa, he'll die," he said. "He was always away in the lakes and the bush. He can barely stay in the reservation house. He lives the old way. He will die, Mondou."

Mondou knew that all the older natives were nomadic and lived the old way. He barely saw them on the reservation. Ox and Snow had told him many stories, and even reassured him that the elder tribesman would check on the Cerf campsite just because they would happen by. Mondou also understood what it was like to be arrested and confined away from home, friends, and family.

"I can't let them take him to Ottawa," Ox said. "If I can set him free, they will never, ever find him again. You drive me close to Maniwaki and let me out. You'll have to lend me the gun for a while. You take Murph, he's too small, and you go where you must go to be safe."

"Ox. I go with you," Murph howled.

They sat in the dark while Mondou worked through his Catholic guilt. Finally he said, "We'll all go north."

As he started the motor, he could hear a distant siren approaching Kaz from the south.

Mondou kept his promise to Ox. Ox's father was the chief of the Algonquin tribe in Maniwaki. He had been arrested on a number of charges, including hiding a zombie gang that traded in alcohol. He was put in the Maniwaki jail to be transported to Ottawa the next day.

Soldiers were sent to Maniwaki and Chief Oxawatik was to be transferred to Ottawa by both soldiers and the QPP.

Just north of Kazabazua, the train was forced to stop because of a large pine that had fallen across the tracks. When the fuss was over, a QPP officer had left the train with Oxawatik and boarded some sort of tank and disappeared into the woods. One soldier was found unconscious and two others barricaded in a washroom. The army made sure that the story was never made public but everyone knew it was the ZombieMan who had dressed as a cop and gotten away with the old chief.

Soon Chief was installed at the Cerf campsite with two warriors and an elder friend, and Mondou had six additional charges against him, including hijacking a train, kidnapping, and two more charges of assault and attempted murder.

Ox came to recognize something in Mondou he had never seen in any man he had ever met. He would say little but in his soul he knew that he must stay by Mondou. If anyone ever tried to capture or kill or even aggravate his brother, they'd have to kill Ox first.

THIRTEEN

August 1947

ON SUNDAY MORNINGS, Marian would sometimes walk down the hill with her little girl once the doors were closed on everyone at the English Mass. She said between preparing the altar for two Masses and sitting through Père's nine o'clock *en français*, God wouldn't mind if she skipped Foley's ten-thirty. Marian would sit and rock and talk with Mac. Then she'd get up and make tea when she knew Mass was about over, and while the tea was steeping, she and Mac would wave at everyone as they drove down the hill from the church.

Aunt Gertie said it made people talk about Marian and Mac, but whenever she mentioned it, Mom would just burst out laughing.

I never went to church unless Mom and Gertie were up for the weekend, and Mom never fussed me about it. Instead, I'd sit on the porch with Mac and Marian, or Mac and I would head to the back porch, twist an old Habitant pea soup can on top of a fence post down by the chicken coop about thirty yards away, and shoot Mac's gun.

Mac would take a tiny bullet out of a small, sleeved box like it was a communion host, insert it into the chamber, raise the gun slowly like a chalice, then take careful aim and fire. Then he'd hand me the gun and I'd do the same thing. After a few times, we'd walk down and check the can, though we pretty well knew when we had good shots because we could hear and see the can go *thunk*.

Sometimes Marian would come to the back porch and shoot with us. She was as good a shot as me.

"Who taught you how to shoot like that?" I asked her once.

She tossed her hair in the direction of the little girl standing behind her on the porch and said, "Her daddy."

When I said, "Who's her daddy?" Mac let out a loud laugh and choked until I thought he was going to blow snot out his nose again.

Marian turned and gave Mac a big long stare and said, "Her daddy is dead, and you, Mac, are an agitator."

"Better than being a reprobate," he answered. I looked up both words because I knew folks called Mac a reprobate and then I understood why Mac would rather be known for "stirring things up" than being a "ne'er do well" or worse.

I also understood why both words would work when folks talked about Mac. What I didn't understand was why nobody seemed sad about the little girl's dead daddy.

On the Sunday after Smoky died, Marian came down the hill as usual. Mac and I were sitting and waiting for the churchgoers to disappear before we went to bury Smoky, who was lying dead in the woodshed.

When Mac saw Marian round the corner of the shop, he got up out of his rocker and stopped her halfway across the front lawn.

"Well, now, me darlin' Marian, you and I need to have a chat out by the shop. Raymond, take Lise back down to the coop and collect the eggs."

I did not want to walk the little girl down to the chicken coop, but by the way he said it, I could tell Mac was feeling mean. Lise could barely walk and could hardly talk yet, but when we got behind the house she looked up at me and said, "Where's Smoky?"

"He's gone," I sobbed, and I started to cry, and Lise ran back to her mother. Then I heard Mac shouting at Marian. Marian was shouting back.

I couldn't believe what I was seeing. Marian put both her hands on Mac's chest and was talking a blue streak.

Finally, Marian shoved away from Mac, picked up her little girl, and started up the hill toward the church.

Mac stood for a while thinking. He looked over in my direction but couldn't see me in the shed window, where I was standing with my hand on Smoky. Then Mac headed up the hill right behind Marian.

I couldn't believe it. My head was screaming, "Mac, leave her alone! Leave it all alone."

Everyone was going crazy. Mac was fighting with the nicest lady in the Gatineau, and Smoky was lying dead in the woodshed.

I couldn't figure anything out. I was feeling so sad and sick. Everything was moving too fast.

As I headed up the hill after Mac, I didn't realize they were about to move faster.

I followed Mac up to the church as cars drove past him down the hill. The English Mass had just finished. Foley and Beaubien would be in the sacristy cleaning up.

Mac limped down to the holy end of the church, staring up at the words that arched over the altar—*My Peace Be Unto You*. I tucked myself into a pew at the back just as the two priests came out and faced Mac at the altar rail.

Mac wasted no time. He looked straight at Father Foley and said, "Who's in the coffin across there with Alfred Mondou's name on the gravestone?"

Father Foley looked surprised at the question.

"If Alfred Mondou's name is on the gravestone, then Alfred is in the coffin, Mac. I'm getting tired of your behaviour and so are many of the parishioners. In fact, there are some of the locals who think you should be committed to an institution. You're wandering around with a rifle and behaving dangerously, and upsetting people by sticking your nose in their business. Why not just leave things alone?"

"That's the second time I've been warned to mind my own business in two days, Father. The first time I was warned through Raymond. Those doing the warning killed his dog, and told him they intended to kill me, and him, too. Kill the boy, for Christ's sake. Do you hear what I'm saying, you dumb assholes?"

Father Foley looked shocked again but not about his language.

"Who would ever threaten to do that, Mac?" he said quietly.

"You tell me, Father. Maybe the person who also knows who's in the coffin."

"Mondou is in that coffin, Mac."

"Then he's a real zombie as Raymond says. He's the walking dead."

"The Mondous have nothing to do with you, old man," Père Beaubien said. "And a zombie is a corpse revived by the devil, monsieur, not a Mondou."

"There are many kinds of zombies, Priest. And I think you two are engaged in criminal acts. It involves folks rising from the dead, or could it be zombies? Criminal activities including theft, and bribery, and . . . probably murder."

Foley went white. "Mac, let's discuss this some other time," he stammered. "Père has no interest in any of this."

"A falsehood, Father. The Mondous are part of Père's parish, not yours. The zombie's funeral Mass was said by Beaubien, not you. I checked. It did happen when I was in Wakefield with my goitre but it was kept damned quiet. And others involved are Irish, Father. That's where you come in—you two are as thick as thieves."

"You are *stupide*," Beaubien said. "Do you hear me, old man? You are a crazy man like they say. Go away from this church. Leave. Get out."

Well, there was one thing Mac knew for sure. He was not *stupide*.

"What do you want, old man?" Beaubien blustered. "Are you just nosy? Do you just like to meddle? Do you not have enough to do? They say you do nothing. Why don't you go back to that instead of bothering everybody? I know by the power of the confessional there has been no murder here," Père Beaubien screamed. "This is all God's will. Go home, old man."

That was enough for Mac. "You know that your zombie did not commit a murder because he told you in the confessional? Are you crazy?"

Beaubien stammered, "That's not what I am saying. You know so little, old man. You don't know what you don't know." And he charged at Mac. Mac backed down the centre aisle of the church. Père was a big man.

"Give your zombie friend this note," Mac said. He handed the note to Father Foley. "I want to see him. And by the way, with the conversations I've had with others, and what I've written down about all this, if me and mine, or even another dog happens to die of curious causes, you two men of the cloth will be wishing you'd died and gone to hell."

At the door of the church, Mac turned to Father Foley.

"A small favour, Father. Raymond's dog I told you about. We'd like to bury him in the back corner of the cemetery, along my lot line. It's important to Raymond."

"Père is right, Mac," Father Foley said, offended. "You are crazy. It is a Catholic cemetery. Consecrated ground. It is man's portal to paradise. You tell me you want to bury a dog there? You're an old fool."

"Oh, Jaysus," Mac moaned.

"Mac, why don't you call on someone you know." It was the kind of comeback Mac normally would have appreciated, but not this time.

He just turned and shuffled out of the church.

We buried Smoky right at the top of the pasture under a tree beside the post-and-wire fence that separated the graveyard from the hayfield.

"Our brave Smoky will have the best view in Christendom, Raymond."

Mac told me to get Smoky's extra bandanas from the farmhouse while he went into the shop. When I got back, Mac was in the shop emptying all his precious writing and ledger from the black woodbox with the big padlock.

"This is the only clean box in here. I'll have to find another spot for my thinking."

Mac took one of the bandanas from me and wrapped it around his own neck. I was doing a quiet cry until then but had to smile at how jaunty Mac looked with his goitre hidden by a red bandana. I put on a bandana, too. We kept Smoky wrapped in Mac's blanket, and then carefully put him in the box.

He fit perfectly.

We put the box on Mac's rumble seat and drove up to the cemetery and turned left onto the faint grass trail that led to the very back of the cemetery.

Mac was carefully winding his way past the gravestones while I was wondering if Father Foley was watching us from the church. Mac turned left at the tall iron cross that stood at the back of the graveyard and carefully inched his jalopy down to the south fence, the side that overlooked the farmhouse and the valley below.

Mac and I trudged along looking through the fence for a perfect spot.

"Look at that, Raymond. It's like a natural gravestone. Flat as a pancake. We'll bury Smoky beside it, and I'll put Smoky and the PX symbol on it later when you're back at school."

We pushed Smoky and the shovels under the wire and then crawled under ourselves. We took turns digging right beside the big flat rock, and Mac said we were putting Smoky in the very spot Mac wanted to be buried, because he could see his home.

I was starting to worry about Mac with all the digging. The veins on his neck above the bandana were rippling like worms. Mac might be lying beside Smoky in his favourite burial spot before we were through. I started to dig longer and harder than Mac.

When we were finished digging, we slipped the box into the hole. We sprinkled dirt on top of the box and said prayers just like Father Foley. Then we finished covering up Smoky's coffin, and I cried again.

As we drove down through the cemetery in Mac's jalopy, we saw Marian standing on her porch. I waved and she waved back, but Mac wouldn't wave.

"Our darlin' Maid Marian is part of the problem," he mumbled. "The doing is his thing, and the thinking is her thing. We'll talk about all that."

I didn't know what he was talking about, but it was getting dark and I was feeling pretty tuckered so I didn't ask any questions. I wanted to be alone to pray for Smoky anyway.

FOURTEEN

February 1945

STILL A CORPORAL, but now based in Ottawa, Grafftey was not happy. He'd been pushed inside because of behaviour unbecoming a soldier in His Majesty's Army. He was in a borrowed office in Number 8 Temporary Building, and he had been assigned the task of running Mondou to ground only because he had pleaded for the assignment. The RCMP, in the midst of a war, had too many similar cases at the time, so Grafftey was resigned to working primarily with the Quebec Provincial Police.

Soon after Mondou's escape, they snooped around Fieldville and Low together simply asking questions. They suspected that Mondou would head home. In mid-December, Grafftey visited the Mondou family farm for the second time and laid down the law. They would arrest anyone harbouring Alfred Mondou. The third time, based on several tips, a coordinated effort was organized to seek out Mondou in two different locations. The RCMP and a couple of military officers would head to Maniwaki and the reservation, where they had jurisdiction, and collect evidence and make arrests if necessary; and Corporal Grafftey would stake out Upper Low with the QPP.

By now, the QPP detested Grafftey. He was a bossy little corporal, yet this wasn't his army. They called him Napoleon.

Nonetheless, they had to take the search for a murderer seriously. *Le ZombieGars* had murdered a policeman.

It was February. Grafftey had promised a few waiters and gas attendants a reward if they heard more about Mondou. That had led to a stakeout. Three QPP cars rushed to Lac Ste. Marie to triangulate on a restaurant-bar across the street from a garage-marina that sat on the edge of the lake. There was a raging blizzard, but through the snow, many in the town saw the three police cars pull in and park in a curious formation. They just sat there. No one got out of any of the cars.

About twenty minutes later, three men in long, white, woollen coats that looked like native garb came out of the restaurant. Instead of turning toward the parking area, the three men marched straight across the road toward the garage on the lake. The first cops to see them shrugged to each other and didn't bother to radio. They just sat tight because the three men were walking toward a garage with nowhere else to go.

The three had almost reached the gas pumps of the station when Grafftey finally saw them from his vantage point in the back seat of the second cruiser, which was parked beyond a snowbank on the bar side of the road. He watched them through the driving snow. He saw them head around the station toward the lake rather than enter the front door of the garage.

It was then that he noticed that one of the men had a black dress swinging below his coat. The man's boots looked army.

"What the fuck is that all about? Get over there!" Grafftey shouted.

By the time the Grafftey cruiser crossed the road and swung into the parking area, the three men had disappeared around the back of the garage. The two other QPP cars pulled in behind Grafftey's cruiser, and everyone got out.

Led by Grafftey, they trudged through drifts into the blizzard blowing off the lake. They were blinded by it.

Suddenly they heard a tremendous roar. To their right something burst onto the frozen ice and started across the lake.

"Get after them. Now! After them! Shoot! For Christ's sake, shoot something!"

The six QPP officers just stood staring at the contraption on the lake. They were mesmerized for a moment, but they sure weren't going to shoot at three unidentified Indians.

"Now—now—into the car! Follow them!"

Grafftey forced his driver and partner into the car and climbed in. They raced around the garage, down the boat launch ramp onto the ice, and went into a three-turn spin, circling with spinning wheels for minutes. The four other officers just watched and laughed. Already their prey was lost in the blinding snow.

The three—Mondou, Murphy, and Ox—headed straight across the lake. Mondou had the SkiTank at full throttle. There was no track faster for his courser than a wide frozen lake.

"Slow down, Mondou. You can't see."

"There's nothing there to see, Murph. Ride 'em, cowboy!"

Five minutes later, the rig hit the far shore with a thud and did what Mondou expected it to do. The skis rode up the bank, and they soared through the air, landing on the lake road, through the far ditch, and headed straight up the mountain.

"You're a crazy fucker, Mondou. I'll tell you that!" Murph shouted as Ox laughed.

A half-hour later, the three police cars had circled the lake by road. Grafftey and the QPP found themselves staring up the hill at the trail leading from the frozen lake. They never even got to see the weird machine disappear as a speck over the crest of the hill far above them. They could still see its tracks, since the blizzard was much less severe on the east side of the lake below the mountain.

"I saw one of those machines in the Townships, where I trained," a QPP officer said. Grafftey didn't hear. He was screaming at them to follow the tracks.

"We have snowshoes in the trunk, Corporal. Follow them if you want. But there are no roads up there, and their tracks will be covered before long. We'd better call ahead."

The QPP officers knew there was no one useful to call. The QPP over the top were on the Francophone side of Quebec's two solitudes, which had always made communication difficult. Furthermore, those detachments would have even less interest in catching a few draft dodgers in the bush. In fact, if they weren't cops, and didn't want to die in the war, they might even want to be part of Mondou's group.

So, despite the fact that Napoleon was throwing a fit, they left their snowshoes in the trunk and told him that they were heading back to Lac Ste. Marie for a nice hot coffee. They sat over coffee for a long time and laughed and shared stories with the locals about the goddamned snow contraption. Grafftey joined them because he had no choice, but he was not laughing. He had just received a call that Mondou had struck again at a bar in Kazabazua and on the rail line just south of Maniwaki. The RCMP and the military had also failed to catch him.

By the day after the blizzard, the story of the big escape had made it all the way down to Wakefield and up to Maniwaki. Between the shooting at the Kazabazua bar, the rescue of Chief Oxawatik, and the Lac Ste. Marie escape, the renegade priest was a local legend. Most people still had no idea who the priest really was, but Grafftey did, and he was not finished yet.

Mondou, Ox, and Murph had lain in the snow in their white woollens at the top of the low mountain, watching the QPP at the bottom of the hill finally decide to give up the search. Mondou peered through binoculars at Grafftey in his army overcoat. He could tell that the man with the wild gyrations would not give up easily. He also guessed that the QPP didn't have their hearts in the job.

All the same, with three police forces and bounty hunters after his blood, he'd have to set up a second base far away from the Gatineau.

Meanwhile, Murph and Ox were rolling in the snow laughing like loonies.

"Have you ever had this much fun sober, Injun?"

Ox just lay on his back heaving his laugh toward heaven. Mondou accepted that he was stuck with his two sidekicks for the rest of the winter. He returned to the job at hand.

He wasn't certain where exactly they should go, but there were no roads anyway. The one road stopped at the end of the line of lake cottages below and would only take them back into Lac Ste. Marie. They had to go east, over the mountains toward the Laurentians.

They looked at their map and circled an area north of a town called Vendée where there was a Quebec park that they knew of called Papineau-Labelle. Alfred thought it might be a good place for another camp. In between, there were more than eighty miles of mountainous bush, some slash fences, areas that had been cleared of timber, and the odd rutted logging roads that were deep in snow.

The next few days would be spent bushwhacking.

When they had time to rest, the three of them laughed about their recent adventures and tried to master a new song, led by Murph on his harp-guitar.

Oh give me land, lots of land, under starry skies above
Don't fence me in.
Let me ride thru the wide-open country that I love
Don't fence me in.

The three fugitives got lucky on the Laurentian side. They found another isolated cave on Lac Cameron and collected more canvas and muslin to set up the camp. Papineau-Labelle Park was even more remote than their Maniwaki camp, and the few year-round locals even less curious about the trappers who wandered into Vendée occasionally. They soon found themselves in business with a local Laurentians trucker who ran goods back and forth to Montreal, which quickly led to other enterprises.

In the spring, the three decided to make a short trip back to Upper Low while there was still enough snow on the ground to travel in the SkiTank. Word had reached Mondou that his family farm had burned down, and he now had money enough to help a little. Ox and Murph were convinced the war was almost over. No one would bother them now.

It was a late April day when the sun shone warm and the Gatineau River flowed timber—when it was summer in the sun and winter in the shade.

Mondou hauled his rowboat up on the west side of the river, leaving Ox and Murph working the shore of the island to the east hauling some logs. There were a lot of rumours about why Mondou was back. He was visiting Père Beaubien and his family, or Ox and Murph wanted to see their families, but nobody knew for sure.

Mondou reached the top of the ridge above the river and started to head northwest when he heard a shout.

"Halt! Stay where you are!"

The apparition of a file of soldiers appearing over the ridge to his left drove Mondou to his right. From the sounds, he knew there were many soldiers. He could see a lead man trying to right his rifle and run at the same time. The soldiers were serious.

Mondou instantly bent low and ran in the direction he was already headed, over the top of the ridge away from the river to the northwest.

The soldiers had been waiting for him. How? Why? Who had told them? He had been careless.

Suddenly there was the sound of a loud crack near his head and another, and another reverberating through the bush, splintering trees. He couldn't get directly back to the river because the soldiers were now between him and his boat.

They had him cornered.

He stayed low, running on the edge of the bush, careful not to be caught in the open. He gradually headed north, extending a long semicircle that would take him back to the river. There were more shots but he didn't hear them ricochet near him.

He knew where he was headed. Less than a quarter mile above the island, he had seen three wide booms of timber on the water. Ox and Murph would have heard all the shooting and would be watching for him from the east side. They would position themselves to pick him up, but he had to get back across the river.

He started to run faster, listening to the shouts of the soldiers recede even farther behind him. He stripped off his heavy wool Indian white as he ran.

He was plunging down the slope of rock and old snow at such a speed that if he lost his balance the chase would be over. Any slower, however, and he'd be an easy target in the water for the soldiers coming over the ridge behind him.

Mondou targeted his final strides for an outcropping of rock hanging several feet over the river. He hit firm with his right leg and dove far out into the Gatineau to reach one of the free-floating logs but avoid the dead heads. He was kicking with boots high as soon as he surfaced, and drove the log toward the first boom.

Then he noticed the cold. The Gatineau was cold.

He did a duck dive to mount the boom in a leap, and now was the time to remember those years of log rolling north of the Paugan. At his best he could bounce across the boom like a balloon blown in a high wind.

He started his bobbing, weaving, shifting run on the water just as the soldiers came over the ridge and started shooting. He had to pray that with all his manoeuvring he was a tough target.

Suddenly he felt logs splintering, and one shot hit his boot while others hissed by his head. The soldiers were anchored in place now, and the shooting was serious.

Without a misstep Mondou made it to the far edge of the first boom. Just as he was about to dive toward a loose log to ride to the second boom, a shot tore through his neck. He finished the plunge but hit the water short of his target. His neck, bloated boots, the weight of his clothes, his legs giving out—something was dragging him under.

Finally he grabbed another log and, for the first time, with his body submerged and his head hidden behind the log, he glanced back at the east shore. Some of the soldiers were running south, probably to board his own boat and give chase. The rest were still shooting.

"Can't quit now." Mondou heaved onto the second boom, his neck and shoulder screaming. If he made it across, he'd be almost out of range of the shooting soldiers. He focused all his energy on making it the best log run of his life. More bullets were thudding into logs, and he felt one sting his ear.

He kept going. It seemed like forever. When he dove into the next space of water, he could see he was too far downstream from the third boom. He was draped over a free log and decided to dump his boots and make for shore. As he started, he could see the SkiTank angling through the trees on the east side.

What a beautiful sight. He was frigid, weak, and had lost all sense of whether the soldiers were still firing. His neck didn't hurt for the moment, but he knew the pain would be back once he was out of the water.

Now he saw Ox standing on the shore waving. Mondou kicked toward his target.

Ox and Murph dragged him out of the river and threw him onto blankets. He sat up and looked across the river, but O'Sullivan's Island was now between them and the soldiers on the far shore. Murph pointed toward three soldiers coming around the south end of the island in Mondou's rowboat. One was rowing, one was in the stern shouting and pointing at Mondou and the third was standing and trying to fire his gun. The Gatineau was dragging the soldiers south, farther away from their target.

Murph stood on a rock outcropping waving at them while he did a little jig and sang: "And it's better to be a zombie/Than a General Service man."

Mondou sat digging through his layers of wet, bloody shirts to find what was lodged at his navel. A piece of his guts, maybe. Out came the silver chain in two pieces with the cross dangling from one.

Ox stared at it and said, "You'd have a gushing hole in your neck if it wasn't for that chain."

❧❀❀❧

As the weather warmed, Mondou realized he needed year-round, off-road transportation. He hauled a Ford truck motor, tractor wheels and seats, and assorted vehicle parts to the Cameron site and began work on a wide-wheeled variation of the JAP tire tank project he had been working on in Terrace. He envisioned a motor machine that could roar through wood clearings and along logging paths when there was no snow on the ground.

The ability to travel the mountain route in all seasons would allow them to set up a third base of operation in the white marble caves behind Baldface Mountain, where they could work the east side of the Gatineau River from Lac Ste. Marie to Wakefield, the same way they could work Maniwaki and Vendée. Mondou started to refer to it as Le Triangle d'Or.

The TireTank project was difficult, because Mondou was starting from scratch. Murph loved repeating to Ox, "This man's too stupid to quit." There was much scavenging of parts to be done, but Ox and Murph were now more helpful, knowing the mobility they had enjoyed on the SkiTank. The fugitives were also left alone. There had been little sign around Cameron of any police effort to find them, which pleased Mondou, who was tired. Tired of running, tired of hiding, tired of grieving.

As summer approached, someone from the other side did find them, however.

"What are you doing here?"

"Whither thou goest, I will go."

Mondou was still mesmerized by the wide, inviting smile.

"How did you find me?"

"Priests can only keep confessional secrets, P'tit."

"It's nice to see you."

"Nice to see you in layman's clothes. A priest in blue jeans."

Mondou just stood there grinning. He had often pictured Marian standing in front of him as she had that Christmas morning, but here, now?

It was too good to be true.

"It's a long way around here. Down to Hull, down the Ottawa River, around and back up into the mountains. It took me a very long day to find you. What brought you here?"

"We came over the top and ran right into it. Much quicker."

"If I can find you, they can, too."

"They'll come from the east end of the lake as you did. There's no other way in. Through Vendée, newcomers making inquiries. Looking curious. We knew you were coming for an hour now. We knew what you were driving. We found you."

They rented a small cottage at the very northwest tip of Lac Sucrerie. It was close to the Cameron camp, and the gravel road dead-ended on the edge of the vast, empty park. The cottage was protected by an enormous hill of rock that overlooked the length of the lake looking toward Vendée.

They called their new home The Rock. There was a large shed built into the base of the rock where Mondou spent the summer finishing his TireTank when he wasn't helping Ox and Murph with the business. Marian was back and forth to the other side three times that summer.

She was also pregnant.

"We like to sleep together, laugh together, work together. We're going to have a baby together. Maybe we should put it together . . . in the church."

Mondou smiled. "*Si tu veux.*"

"No, you have to wish it, too. Just say, *Oui, ma jolie.*"

"*Oui, ma jolie.*"

Ox and Murph enjoyed the slower pace now that Marian was burning Mondou's energy. One day while sitting in the pines at the top of The Rock, drinking quarts and looking down over the lake, Murph stood up and used the binoculars. He scanned the lake like a captain on the bridge of a ship.

He stopped and focused on one spot for a long time.

Ox, who was almost asleep, peered up at Murph.

"What do you see?" he said.

"A great view. I'm watching Marian and Mondou do what no other two could do."

"And what would that be?"

"Screw in a canoe."

Dressed in casual civilian clothes, Corporal Grafftey walked into The Ottawa House, a tavern just across the Chaudière Bridge in Hull. He found an isolated table near the back wall, partially hidden by the small bandstand. The bar smelled of stale beer and cigarettes.

Munro came through the door twenty minutes later and stood near the doorway while his eyes adjusted. Then he saw Grafftey wave. He shook his head, as if he was surprised Grafftey was there, and then walked toward the table through the smoke circling in the dim light from the window.

Grafftey noticed that Munro's left arm was hanging differently as he approached, and he remembered that Munro was left-handed. It was the kind of detail that Grafftey remembered about all the conscripts in Petawawa.

As Munro sat, he swung his red left hand onto the table with an enormous thud, loud enough to draw a mean glance from the bartender.

Grafftey nodded at the red hand and said, "Why'd you choose red instead of a nice khaki? It certainly catches the eye."

"Blood, Grafftey. It reminds me that I need blood." Munro

rolled the leaden hand over and back. "This is the Red Hand of Ulster."

A shout came from the bartender peering over the bandstand. "Hey, *voulez une draft*?"

"*Oui, deux, s'il vous plaît*," Grafftey shouted back.

"I came all the way down from Wakefield, so you're buying," Munro said.

Grafftey nodded and then started his monologue.

"After you left Petawawa I continued our work. Getting those chickenshits to the war. If it makes you feel better I was reprimanded a few times by those political H.Q. assholes that got you. Last month they took my stripe and sent me back to Ottawa."

"Something I said makes you think I give a shit about any of this, Grafftey? I'm here to hear about Mondou."

The bartender approached with the beer, slammed it down, and said, "Waiters aren't back until five. You want more, come to the bar."

Munro spoke before Grafftey could continue.

"You've got the army and the cops. Why do you need me?"

"The QPP don't really want to catch him. I suspect they're helping him. The RCMP are always fuckin' me around about jurisdiction. If it ain't about the reserve up in Maniwaki, they don't move. The army will move if we have a target and a plan. They're not going up there on any wild goose chases." Grafftey didn't say "any *more* wild goose chases," because after two false starts, the army was wary of Grafftey's vendetta. There were thousands of zombies who would never be accounted for, and the army was coming to accept that they'd all be pardoned someday.

"I've heard about your raids up there, Grafftey. No luck? I'm not surprised."

"That's why I need you," Grafftey said. "I also know you're in the zombie business. If you help me track him, I'll get the men and we'll get this guy hanged."

"First of all, I'm not a bounty hunter, Grafftey. I prefer to be called a vigilante. And secondly, I will kill Mondou long before you get to hang him. I'm going to find the fucker, chop off his hands and then shoot him a dozen times. I don't need you."

"Do you know where he is, Munro? Do you know about his camps? I know more about him than you, or anyone else in the country. Did you know he's hanging around the Laurentians, which is why you haven't found him yet? We'll do better together."

"What do you want?"

"You're an insider up there. With what I provide you, you'll know who to convince that they should help us find out when and where he'll be back. He's been back since he shot you in Kazabazua. He has lots of friends and disguises and locations, but home base for him and his gang is under your nose. Help me, and I guarantee that if we get him while he's still wanted for murder no one will charge you for killing him. It's a free shot."

Munro squinted, "Isn't there a reward involved? That would come in handy. Helps convince folks whose side they should be on."

"You see? You do need me. I can also deliver the reward." Grafftey smiled and raised his glass.

"The war is almost over. Why do you give a shit about one zombie? He didn't shoot off your hand."

"Because he has no respect. Not for our country or our war. He killed a man to avoid doing the right thing, and nobody gave a shit. It's not right."

Munro suspected he knew Grafftey's real reasons: Mondou had no respect for Grafftey, or his uniform, and Grafftey wasn't going to take that from a frog zombie. Also, Grafftey was probably deluded enough to think the army would see him differently if he finally caught the criminal who had ruined his career.

"Okay, Grafftey. A cat doesn't dislike what it tries to kill but we both owe this bastard for our own reasons. Let's catch him . . . and kill him."

Finally, Munro lifted his glass in a toast.

Mondou, Père Beaubien, and Father Foley were having a meeting. There were two items on the agenda. One was Mondou's funeral. The other was his wedding.

Beaubien said, "Now, Mondou, you and I have to agree that you are not going to wed this woman. You must get rid of that Irish Madonna-whore."

"And I'm not going to participate in a funeral Mass for a man who's not dead and pretend that I'm doing it to offer up prayers for your nameless cadaver, Père," Foley responded. "Is the man you'll be burying in our hallowed ground even a Catholic?"

Both priests knew each other well. They understood they were equal halves of an unfortunate partnership. Foley knew that Beaubien was kind to those who revered him, but the Indian, Irish, Mondou, and especially the whore, had seemingly not placated Père properly, given all he had done for them. Murph called Beaubien their Friar Tuck.

Mondou knew that Beaubien was a very strange priest. Not devout like Foley, but a strong man, intelligent, an organizer. Beaubien used his parishes with power, Foley walked the roads with his breviary.

Foley also suspected that Beaubien looked upon Foley himself as a bit of a simpleton, but Foley was that rare priest who really cared about only one opinion, and it wasn't Père's.

Foley liked being simple. It made his life simple. He would try again to simplify for Beaubien.

"Marian, her mother, and her family are faithful members of Holy Mother Church, Père. There's no reason to damn Marian to a life of sin with fatherless children. Our Lord would not want her sin to continue. And in this parish, it's better to be married to a fugitive than not at all," Foley said quietly.

"Father, Mondou's funeral was my idea in the first place, and now, thanks to God's gracious gift, we can bury him with his identity. I must do that for him or he will be a fugitive forever. If the poor departed corpse is buried in Alfred Mondou's name, he would be Catholic, would he not? What you are trying to do with this marriage, however, will destroy my efforts. The authorities will wonder how a dead man could marry. We cannot risk that."

Beaubien had made his move but he knew his Father Foley, and he also knew what he, himself, would say in the same situation.

"You and I know that it is only important to be married in the eyes of God and the Holy Mother Church, Père. Nothing need be sent to the government. For more than a thousand years our Church was all the government necessary for a true marriage. This is the same. If, someday, Mondou is no longer a fugitive and he wants to show some bureaucrat his papers from St. Martin's, then so be it. In the meantime, Alfred and Marian want to proceed with both ceremonies."

"You will read the banns to an empty church, Father?"

"I already have, Père. Three times, and I'll do so three more times, if you wish." Foley smiled, wrinkling his balding forehead.

"So, it's decided, then," Beaubien sighed. "You marry them and I'll bury him. I think, good Father Foley, that mine is by far the greater sin."

"Mine is no sin at all," said Foley. "Your sins, however . . . the list is a long one: an unclaimed corpse that will remain unidentified to family and friends, wherever they are; a poor soul who met his maker who knows how; altered documents; and a web of lies. There must be more than venial sins in that collection. Lord have mercy on your soul. Even worse, you'll probably be proud of it after it's done." Foley started to laugh. "And, yes, I will hear your confession, *si tu veux.*" *Even though a clear-thinking God would charge me with aiding and abetting*, he thought.

Beaubien acted shocked and then grunted, "I think that's the first time I've seen you laugh, Father. You should do it more often. They say it's good for the soul. In any case, this all started because of me and my zombie, and I must finish it, the sooner the better. I'm confident that I will feel true regret for my sins once they are behind me so that God through my priest will suggest a penance and grant me absolution." Beaubien paused. "Father, it occurs to me that we will not know whether to pray that Mondou should rest in peace, or that he should love, honour, and obey."

Foley laughed again along with Beaubien. *So this is honour among thieves*, he thought.

The Church custom was to conduct funerals on a weekday and weddings on Saturday, which was why Mondou was mourned on a Friday and married the day after. The Martindale church was chosen not only because it was Marian's home parish and like most country churches was directly across from a graveyard, but because, unlike all other churches in the Gatineau, it was not situated in town. It was also far from Fieldville and too many nosy Mondou neighbours. Although Martindale happened to be the home of Mac Gleason, known as the nosiest man in the Gatineau, Father Foley had been informed that Mac was near death in the Wakefield hospital. St. Martin's Church and graveyard were therefore perfect.

Mondou participated in his funeral dressed in his priestly garb—both as a caution to protect his identity, and because as once a long-serving altar boy, he knew the funeral ceremony well. Without Foley, Beaubien needed assistance to ensure the Mass for the Dead with closed coffin, and the rare winter procession to the graveyard went smoothly.

Mondou's brother and sisters and a half-dozen close relatives from Fieldville attended the funeral. They could all be trusted under pain of everlasting Père Beaubien to mourn appropriately in front of the watching undertaker, gravediggers, and whoever else should happen by.

Proulx did happen by. He was known to haunt the church, rarely missing any event including benedictions and weddings, but he was particularly fond of funerals.

Looking out from the sacristy, Mondou said, "Père, how would Proulx even know about our funeral?"

"Do not worry about Proulx," Père said. "He has been a great help in our endeavour."

The funeral went well except for mean looks from the two gravediggers and undertaker, who did not seem happy conducting an unprecedented winter funeral at the top of the windiest hill in Upper Low.

As the cortege led by Père Beaubien solemnly shuffled through snow back toward the church, his brother Marc peeked back at him, and then did a little boot jig that made Alfred laugh. Marc was hurling a challenge. Alfred could never tap like Marc, but tonight he'd work up a sweat trying.

Everyone compensated for their self-control through the funeral by getting rip-roaring drunk at Mondou's wake and bachelor party that night at the family farm near Fieldville. Ox and Murph had not been invited to the funeral because they were too conspicuous, but they could not be denied the party.

Père Beaubien left the party before the stupidity started, and the battle of the brothers began. Like the old days, they put a chair in the centre of the kitchen table for Uncle Rudolf, the fiddler. Two other uncles, Oscar and Albert, sat in chairs against the wall with their spoons on their knees, with Uncle Leo standing beside them with spoons raised high in his right hand like a flamenco dancer. Marc brought Alfred their father's shoes with taps on the heels and toes, and then put on his own. The fiddle fired, and was quickly joined by the clickety-click clatter of the spoons, the clapping of the onlookers, and the earsplitting sound of the shoes on a ten-foot square plank sitting on the hardwood floor. Inside, it was earsplitting. Outside, folks would have heard the ruckus from miles away. Marc and Alfred danced for well over an hour without stop, until Mondou's calves finally had to concede.

"So much for army training," his brother laughed.

At the very end of the evening, Mondou found Ox and Murph collapsed on the earthen floor of the cellar beside the stacked bottles of family wine, alcool, and brandy. Mondou dragged a tarpaulin down from the overhead beams, spread it out, rolled Ox and Murph onto the tarp, and then covered them with the ends—two drunken bugs in a rug. Throughout his efforts, Ox grunted while Murph was slurring continuously in some old Irish argot that Mondou could barely understand.

"Can't fall from down here now, can I, boss. As low as we can go down here. Lower than Low. Oh . . . across the sea to Ireland . . . heh. Tanks for the party, boss. You're a great boss. A great zombie. Sad to be buried without your head, though. Was the head an Irish one, do ya t'ink? Even a zombie should have a head. If ya ever want to bury your head 'long wit' the rest, I know where it is, boss."

Murph then fell unconscious.

The next morning at the wedding at St. Martin's, there were a number of suffering souls, while Murph and Ox contentedly slept off their hangovers at the Mondou farmhouse.

As he waited for his flock to arrive at the wedding, Father Foley found himself looking down at Mac's house below. He was haunted by the possibility that the old man would rise from his sickbed and make an appearance. There was also the prospect of Mac's death. It was not so much Mac's death but the thought of administering Mac Gleason last rites at the Wakefield hospital that caused Foley anguish. As a registered parishioner it was Foley's solemn duty to pray over the man on his deathbed but he found himself hoping Dr. Barbee would not call until Mac was unconscious. Getting a host into Mac's mouth after trying to get him to confess his sins would likely cost Foley a finger.

Finally, by 10:45, the Mondou clan and Marian's parents and sisters were huddled in front of the altar at St. Martin's.

There were many amusements at both the wedding and the reception held that afternoon at Marian's family home up the road from St. Martin's. An important highlight at the church was the groom in priest's garb turning to kiss the pregnant bride.

By mid-February, the news, officially and otherwise, had spread that Mondou was dead—found under an ice-fishing hut beneath a hole that was being axed on Lac Ste. Marie, presumably many months after the poor man had drowned. Somehow he had lost his head. It was suspected that the ice fishers and their spud bar were responsible for the missing head. The body was identified as being that of Alfred Mondou, and the funeral was properly recorded in Quebec City and Ottawa.

Grafftey was relieved, but Munro was angry. He would have liked to be the one to remove Mondou's head.

FIFTEEN

August 1947

I WAS TIRED, but I couldn't sleep that night. I knew Mac couldn't either because I could hear his rocker creaking longer than usual.

I got up and looked out the window, which faced north up the hill. I could see the graveyard cross and the church steeple, and I said prayers for Smoky. Soon crazy colours were dancing in the sky, streaking up from the horizon. I'd seen the Northern Lights before but they were never as spectacular as this night. Rippling reds and greens with surges of flashing white leaping up from Smoky's new grave.

God was having a welcoming party for Smoky.

Mac's rocking chair stopped squeaking just as I noticed someone coming down the hill through the field from the graveyard, the lights streaming behind him.

A zombie.

He disappeared into the gully. I was about to shout a warning just as Mac appeared beneath my window with his gun. He was moving to intercept the zombie. I tried but couldn't scream, like I was in the middle of a nightmare.

When the zombie surfaced again, Mac shouted, "Stop or I'll put a bullet between your eyes."

The zombie put his hands in the air and answered, "You sent for me."

"You're ZombieMan?"

The visitor laughed. "Well, I'm Mondou. ZombieMan, *si tu veux.*"

"Are you armed?"

"No."

"Do you want some tea?"

"No, thank you."

"A beer?"

"No."

"Good, because I don't have any. Well, come sit down."

When I was certain that they were sitting on the porch rockers, I quietly stole down to my listening post.

". . . the dog was an accident," ZombieMan was saying. "It was them that was there that night, all right. The Irish is small and quick, the Algonquin the opposite. He's huge. I've never seen such a strong man as Ox. And he doesn't know the full of it. Strange, too, he loves animals. He's good with them. They were both drunk, which they do when I'm busy with others. When Ox heard the dog died, he cried. I don't know what else to tell you."

"Nothing more to me. Maybe to the boy, someday." Mac horked one of his spits out onto the lawn.

"The ChiRho symbol works, I guess. It got you here," Mac said.

"The symbol has been very useful for our garrison, but we have many ways of communicating. It's not really why I came. I owe you a favour from many years ago so I don't want to fight you. Do you remember me?"

"Yes."

"No other Irish in the Gatineau would have picked up my father from the ground in front of the Paugan and driven him all the way into Fieldville. I remember you pulling up in front of the porch with Père's legs hanging over the edge of your rumble seat like it happened last night."

"And I remember you on your porch and your brother and

mother, Mondou. You look just like your father. How old were you then?"

"Maybe nine, ten. Père was a good man, Mac."

"I know, Mondou, I know."

No one talked for a while. There was only the creaking of rockers, the sounds of bats and crickets.

"I read something in the *Ottawa Journal* a while back about you zombies," Mac said after a while. "Somebody said when you were called up to serve overseas, you'd all disappear into the woodwork like cockroaches when the light comes on. But a bunch of bandit zombies running around less than an hour from Ottawa? The bloody capital, the Parliament buildings, army headquarters, the Supreme Court. Right under their nose. It's a wonder."

"Life is local, Mac. Many locals, even in the QPP, hate everything down the river. Père Beaubien, Marian, and I worried most about you. The way we saw it, in the Gatineau, if you didn't know about it, it didn't happen. I was buried, my death filed in Ottawa, my name put on the gravestone. And it worked. Then you dug out the truth and now the hounds are on my trail again."

Marian?

"Heh, heh, heh." I could hear Mac squirt tobacco juice out onto the lawn.

"There are zombies and evaders even closer to Ottawa than us, Mac. Down at Wolf Lake, and in from Wakefield. But Ottawa wants me a lot worse than any of them."

"Which brings us right to the point, Mondou. If you wanted to kill people, you shoulda gone to the war. I fought a better war than you sitting here on my porch."

"*Bon, Monsieur* Mac, but in my world, to go to their war was a sacrilege. To not go was to be cursed. There was no pure path."

"You found one. You ran away."

"No, I walked away. It was stand at the top of that hill in the lightning or come inside. Come home."

"Well, I think you should have fought the good war."

"Tell me how to do that now."

Mac squirted more juice. "Well, it was a good thought until I heard me say it."

"It's *fait accompli*, Mac. I missed that war that we hear so much more about now . . . the atrocities, the Jews, and the death camps. It would be good to have helped conquer the Satan Hitler, but I missed it. I'm not dead but I pay a price. There are consequences to all the choices God grants us. But I just can't let this war continue for me."

"There will always be the misery of this thing undone for you, Mondou."

There was only the sound of the creaking rockers for a while.

"For years, I thought you were a fable. Now, here you are. Tell me about your murders."

"I haven't murdered anyone."

"You murdered a CN policeman."

"I was pushing him out of my way. I was a prisoner who committed no crime."

Again there was the creaking of rockers for a while.

"It says *Je sais qu'il vit* on your gravestone. You do live; so who's in your coffin? If there's a body in there, it will be murder number two."

"It's some of our Gatineau rocks."

"It's not rocks. I have an undertaker who'll swear to that. So who is it?"

Both rockers stopped creaking. It was so quiet for so long that I found a way to peek over the sill to see the two of them.

"What has any of this got to do with you?"

"You may have killed my brother," Mac answered.

"Somebody killed your brother?"

"No, I don't have a brother, but it's somebody's brother or father or husband. It's someone who is missing, and murdered."

The ZombieMan finally sighed and said, "The body was

a stranger who worked by the river, I was told. He was found washing up against McGoey Dam. That's all I know."

"What do you mean that's all you know? You don't know that he got in your coffin instead of you, and was buried at your funeral with your name on his headstone?"

"Yeah. I know all of that, too. It seemed like a smart idea to bury me so the police would stop looking. I could live my life. I'm the one they want most, and it was affecting too many up here. If I was gone, it would be easier for everyone. It was a closed casket because after a long time in the river it was a poor-looking thing."

"So it was all your idea?"

"We were going to have to bury him anyway. Père Beaubien planted the idea when he mentioned there was a rumour going around that I was dead. If I was officially dead, they would leave me alone."

"Why not your hometown church at Fieldville?"

"Too close to home, lots more questions, relatives, risks. You were the one risk in Martindale, and sure enough, you've become a pain in the arse. Father Foley warned us about you."

"Why didn't you put a death date on the gravestone?"

"It's on all the official papers, but I couldn't do it. First, it seemed like it would be a curse. Then we didn't get around to it. Finally, it didn't matter anymore."

"Why do you keep coming back to visit the grave?" asked Mac.

"Have you ever participated at your own funeral, Mac? Heard your name being repeated as they're throwing dirt on your casket—'Grant Alfred Mondou everlasting rest, O Lord, and let perpetual light shine upon him, with thy Saints, for Thou art merciful.' It's strange, Mac. And then you stand beside your grave and watch yourself being lowered into it. And Beaubien sprinkling holy water. Then your gravestone standing there with your name on it. I vowed that I would pray for the man who died alone, and pray for myself, I guess. It's like looking

back from death. I visit when I can. When I'm at St. Martin's."
He paused. "Remember, this man died that I might have life."

There was a great guffaw from Mac.

"You've got a God complex. So, be like Jesus. Tell the truth. It'll set you free."

"The truth will do the opposite. It will imprison me. Or worse. Our military executed a soldier only two years ago. On the last day of the war. And I face more charges than him, *sacrement*."

"What's more important than the truth, Mondou?"

"Hope is more important. The truth is we'll all die soon. Do you think it's important that you should focus on the truth that you'll be a drooling, brain-dead old man not able to feed yourself with no wife, no children, and no one who gives a shit about you? We'll probably smell your corpse in here from the road. If we lived with the truth of everything, the misery would ruin the life we've got left. Charity, faith, hope for this day. They're all more important than truth."

"Well, all that about smelling my corpse from the road ain't too charitable."

"If you think the truth is that I should be in jail, then who will take care of all the people I now take care of? *Le syndicat* has more dependants than the Quebec government. It's the truth that I should have taken my chances and gone to war when I was first conscripted, and be dead or done with this now. But I didn't. What good is that old truth? The truth now is that I have responsibilities. My people are more important than an old truth from the war. Some say I should get what I deserve. First, they are very wrong about what I deserve. Second, those assholes in Ottawa will never figure out what I deserve. Third, it would be a tragedy if we all got what we deserved, Mac. Let God judge that."

"That's quite a speech, Mondou. You've been practising that, I'll bet," Mac answered. The zombie said nothing.

"So how do you support yourself and all your dependants?" Mac asked.

"Zombie Industries is quite a business. Winter, we've got lots of trees pumping out maple syrup, and we gather it a lot more efficiently than the horse teams. We do honey in the summer. The timber business is good year-round. We do some building, some of it government funded." He laughed. "We run some booze and cigarettes through Montreal. Steal from the rich and give to the poor. As Murph says, there are a dozen illegal ways to make an honest living."

Mac laughed.

"Mac, did you know that a soldier's wife or widow gets sixty dollars a month, and many never got it, and others finally got it when it was too late for their families?"

"You're quite thoughtful for a bandit, Mondou."

"Thank you, Old Mac."

Mac said, "Okay, so what's your plan for me? Ask me to sit here and ignore the whole thing? Kill me?"

The ZombieMan turned in the rocker to face Mac. I had to duck a little.

"You know that story you tell everyone about the crows throwing you a rope when you fell in the well? If we'd wanted to kill you, we would have let you drown that night."

Mac said nothing.

"I was visiting *ma jolie* at the priest's house. Ox was standing guard as usual. He saw you down at the back barn in the twilight. Then you disappeared. The crows started to kick up a fuss. A thousand of them diving and cawing right into the darkness. Our Ox knows his crows. It wasn't their pattern. When I came out, we walked through the cemetery and down to the back barn. Heard your shouting, found the rope in the barn, tied it to the tree and tossed it down. Then we hid and listened to you coughing and grunting until you made it up."

Mac spat some more tobacco juice. "You just ruined my best story."

"It's still a true story. If it hadn't been for the crows . . . Now, let's talk about us. Help me find a way out. Be a friend. I can help you. I'm your neighbour. You can help me. But don't tell me to go down to Ottawa and surrender and rot in jail and hope that someday the politicians will find a way to forgive me."

Mac said, "Amnesty."

"Amnesty, clemency, a pardon, it's bullshit, and it will never happen for me. All that matters is God's forgiveness."

There was a pause and then Mac said, "Your Maid Marian is looking particularly beautiful these days."

"Yes, she's pregnant again. Rumour has it that you're the cause."

Mac laughed and laughed until he went into a coughing and spitting fit. "Oh, Lord, ain't life strange, Mondou? Anyway, what happens if you're caught?"

"They won't catch me. They were never very good at it. I haven't been hit in a while. As long as I don't rub their noses in it. They used to predict that I'd disappear like a cockroach. Now the authorities want it to happen. But you're causing trouble, stirring it up again."

"So you live with this hanging over you forever," said Mac.

"Tell me another way, Mac." Mac said nothing for a while and they rocked.

"Well, I have torment, Alfred. But if helping you is wrong, then I don't want to be right. And I've wasted enough of your time. You're wrong about them not caring about catching you anymore. Corporal Grafftey from Ottawa and some army types have teamed up with that fella they call Mad Munro. They call you their extinction project. I'm not sure they're official."

"You're right. If the QPP knew about it, I would know."

"They say you can judge a man by his enemies. You picked two of the worst."

"I need nine lives to escape those two. And they burned down half our family farm. I hear Munro loves playing with fire. So I've got a lot of friends who need protecting from him. How do you know they're going to attack me?"

At that point, Mac stopped his rocker, and I peeked over the sill again. Mac had his elbows locked on his knees, and his eyes locked on ZombieMan.

"Well, last night down at the Paugan someone tried to find out what I know, and somehow he got to thinking that I'd join up with them. Never send a drunk to do a sober job, Alfred. Booze is a bad partner. I guess you've learned that. This drunk got to talking. He said they'd hit your camp soon, and you and the Indian and the Irish would be dead men."

"Which camp?"

"How many have you got?"

"You be careful, Old Mac. They'll make short work of you if they think you're a problem for them. Or if they think you can lead them to me."

"Don't worry about me. If it wasn't for worrying about Raymond, I'd be having so much fun I wouldn't trade it for a pension. And most folks around here know I'm a harmless old fool, so I'll be fine. No, I want to thank you for coming here with your side of the story. It helps me do the right thing. Letting mad dogs murder you is not the right thing."

"The boy's here, isn't he."

"Upstairs in bed. We buried his dog today. We'll get him right back to the city where he'll be safe."

"Good. I'll make sure someone's watching the place. You've given me important information, and I have much to do. I'm best when I have much to do. I can muzzle these mad dogs. We'd make a good team. Your brains and my brawn."

I saw ZombieMan stand and reach over and shake Mac's hand.

Mac stood up and they walked toward the road together as I heard Mac laughing and sounding very friendly with Zombie-Man, and that's when it hit me.

They might not be like movie zombies, but these ones killed people and dogs. Mac was switching sides. Joining their team.

Smoky was still dead. And the zombies killed him.

I was so sad thinking of Mac changing sides like he did.

Could you be so lonely that you'd join a zombie gang? And where did that leave me?

Nowhere, that's where.

I woke up early, curled beside the wall of the parlour under the window. There was a pillow under my head and I was covered with a blanket.

I turned and saw Mac cracking eggs over the big skillet on the stove. I realized he knew that I'd been snooping on him and ZombieMan.

"Good morning, Raymond. You pick the queerest places to sleep."

I dragged over to the table with the blanket and tried to change the subject.

"Are we having eggs?"

"Yep, and some thick bacon and beans, and then we're going to sit down and have a chinwag. You've got some catching up to do. Over breakfast you can tell me how much you heard last night. Then I'll fill in the rest."

I got the wire rack and started doing toast over another hole in the stove. We had the best breakfast ever, while I told Mac what I'd heard. Then Mac put the dishes in a square hole that held hot water in the back of the stove, and walked over to the secretary desk and pulled out the tall, wide book with the papers hanging out that I saw him working on in the shop.

He sat down with all of it and then said, "Jaysus, my mind is goin'. Raymond, go get the dictionary."

Mac then told me to sit across from him. He pointed at the dictionary and said, "This is the best place to start. Have you ever looked up your zombies in the dictionary, Raymond?"

I shook my head.

"Those Oxford fellows are smarter than I thought," Mac said. "You read it to me."

"Number 1, 'In the West Indies and southern states of America, a soulless corpse said to have been revived by witchcraft; formerly the name of a snake-deity in voodoo cults of or deriving from West Africa and Haiti.' Number 2, 'A dull, apathetic or slow-witted person. Also as a general term of disparagement.' Number 3, 'Canadian military slang. In the war of 1939–45, an oppro . . . oppro—'"

"Opprobrious, Raymond. Opprobrious. It means abusive or insulting. An abusive or insulting term."

"'—an insulting term applied to men conscripted for home defence.' Number 4. 'A long mixed drink—'"

"You see? The Oxford folks defined your zombies, the soulless kind that are walking dead but now they've added the soulless Canadians who signed up but refused to go over to fight in the war. They're only considered walking dead as an insult. So—"

"They're not corpses from graves? They're not dead people?"

"No."

Mac was busy shuffling paper around.

"This is an old ledger where I've been sticking notes for a long while. Notes about lots of things. Just so I'd have them clear in my mind. There's writing here about the zombies because they are the queerest stories I've come across in a long time. I should have told you some of this a couple of days ago when it all started, but no one wants to talk about war zombies. They don't care if you know about movie zombies that aren't real, but they don't want you to know about war zombies that are. No one wants to admit there are men in the bush hiding from the war. They're an embarrassment to Canada. And nobody knows what to do with them now that the war is over, and them that's hiding don't know what to do with themselves. Some are criminals. They've had to do some bad things to survive."

"Like real graveyard zombies?"

"No. Just stealing and stuff to stay alive. Not killing. Anyway, just lately, there was an amnesty. Sort of like a general absolution by the priest, but that didn't apply to some and was too late for others. Some disappeared from the wartime work they were doing here in Canada, some broke wartime regulations, or the law. Some local authorities didn't have to give pardons, and others didn't give them out of spite." Mac stopped and took a couple of puffs from his pipe. I watched the smoke curl above him.

Finally, Mac said, "Do you understand, Raymond?"

"Yeah. I understand. The zombie who was here last night. His gang didn't go to war and die like others, and they killed Smoky and they all got away with it. That's a . . . a rotten sin!" I think I yelled the last part.

"Well, I opened your spigot and you poured out for sure," Mac nodded. "The ZombieMan is no saint but he's not a sinner. I like him, Raymond, so I've decided to have faith in him." Mac stopped and stared at me. I didn't answer. I just stared down at my feet.

"You need to have faith in something," Mac sighed. He spread his ledger flat on the table and seemed to be thinking hard.

"We'll have to find a better home for our secrets, Raymond. Gertie would have a fit over half of this, and the other half she'd spread like manure. It's all rotting away in the shop, and the girls will find it in here for sure."

The last time I saw the collection that day, it was still spread across the table with the elastic bands sitting on top of everything.

SIXTEEN

August 1947

MUNRO LOOKED OVER at Popeye, who was driving the new Ford Flathead they had bought with the money raised trafficking in stolen goods and drugs. He could read most of the tattoo on Popeye's right forearm straddled across the steering wheel: *Teeth Bared*. The tattoo on Popeye's left forearm read: *Nothing Spared*.

Munro smiled as he pictured Popeye's favourite routine—standing in a bar, rolling his sleeves up to display his massive Popeye forearms, slamming his fists together and hollering at the patrons, "Teeth Bared, Nothing Spared." Then his big face would grin to flaunt his hideous teeth, like dog fangs, each one separated from the next across his huge mouth.

Popeye swore that he sharpened his teeth with a file. Munro had never seen him do it but accepted the story for its scare value. He wondered how many battles they had won because Popeye, like a gorilla with bad teeth, was standing beside an even bigger man with an iron red hand—a twosome too gruesome to defy.

Popeye was elated when Munro suggested they form a gang just after the war and call themselves the Popeyes, and thereafter Popeye yielded to Munro's good judgment as "boss."

Not long after, they were approached by a biker gang out of

Montreal, coincidentally also called the Popeyes. "They stole our name," Popeye told everyone.

The two groups met in Hull, and then later in Montreal, and the proposition was to establish Munro and Popeye as the western Quebec affiliate. They were given useful links to a burgeoning drug business and contact points in Montreal.

Munro agreed to all the terms except the question of transportation.

"As long as we can use trucks and not Harleys. You know how fuckin' cold it is here nine months of the year." The Popeyes didn't care how their affiliates travelled.

"Head over the Chaudière to Ottawa," Munro said. All the way up Wellington, he kept repeating what he'd been saying for days.

"I knew Mondou was alive. I knew he was behind the shit we've been hearing about the zombie gang. Two fucking years he's been running loose after blowing off my hand. And everybody probably knew it but us. *ZombieGars*, my ass. And just when we're close, that idiot Grafftey says he's dead. A year and a half wasted with crafty Grafftey . . . hey, pull a right on Metcalfe and then stop before Sparks."

Popeye, as was his way with Munro, just followed the instructions and said nothing.

"Look at this, Popeye. I could step out of this rig, walk across a ten-foot sidewalk into the lobby of the American embassy, and shoot me a big-shot ambassador."

Munro leaned forward and patted the butt of his rifle. He had wanted to mount their guns on a rack behind the seat of their truck but knew it would only aggravate nosy Chelsea neighbours and the police. He built a holster instead. It ran behind his calves across the seat bench. It couldn't be seen, but when he leaped from the truck, he could easily reach the butt of the gun and draw the barrel smoothly into action.

When Popeye saw the manoeuvre, he wanted a sleeve installed on the driver's side as well. Munro was happy to oblige.

"Ya hear me? I could walk up there to Parlyment and blow all those arseholes to hell, and no security to stop me but a near-dead commissionaire who probably never fought in any fuckin' war. I thought about doing that all the time I was delivering telegrams. All you need in Ottawa is a uniform. Doesn't matter what kind. Delivering the telegrams, they give you a smart jacket with shiny buttons, peaked cap, and spats for all the biking, and you can walk into the prime minister's and blow his fucking head off. Easy pickings, Popeye."

Popeye turned the truck onto Metcalfe.

"Pull up before the corner and park. Pull onto the sidewalk if you have to. I'll be in and out of there in ten minutes. The teleyguys will remember me for sure."

Munro strutted down a back alley littered with bicycles behind the CNR telegraph office that sat at the corner of Sparks Street. True to his word, he was back within ten minutes wearing a dark grey cap that made him look like a train conductor. He was also carrying a jacket with silver buttons that matched his hat.

"Drive, Popeye," Munro said as he waved a sheet of paper and an envelope. "Grafftey gets too many telegrams to think he can hide. He's in Temporary Number 8 on Elgin Street and he'll regret the fucking day he wouldn't return my calls."

Popeye spoke for the first time.

"What makes you think he'll come with us?"

"Well, if the dumb fuck is not impressed with my news that Mondou is not dead, then I've got a hundred things on him that will move his sorry arse. He don't have a choice. He'll help us find him, all right. Old Mac Gleason has been talking all over Low about Mondou not being in the grave. If Grafftey in his bullshit army duds don't get him to talk, Old Mac isn't gonna get much older. And if Grafftey's with us when we kill that phony priest, zombie arsehole, we'll be cleared. Official army business. Anyway, I don't give a shit one way or the other. You can't be charged for killing a dead man."

SEVENTEEN

August 1947

I WAS BEGINNING to hate graveyards, but I made a vow to myself that I would visit Smoky's grave every day before I went back to Ottawa, and there were only a few days left. It was easier to walk up the road, turn into the cemetery, and then kneel by the post and wire fence praying over the grave than to struggle up through the crop of oats that Uncle Martin had planted on the hill.

When I moved to the top of the hill, I could hear some folks talking. As I peered over the rise at the top of the hill, I saw the gravediggers at the north edge of the graveyard. They seemed to be leaving so they must have just finished digging the hole for John Doyle, Low's old mayor who had just died.

Smoky was all right where he was on the edge of the cemetery. Mac's bush on the west was separated from the cemetery only by a rotting timber log fence, and on the south side by a dozen posts and wire, so you could hardly tell whether Smoky was in or out.

I skirted along the south wire fence to the back corner and knelt down with my head resting on a fence post and admired Smoky's grave. Then I started to pray.

I saw the approach of the truck for a long time from the far end of the valley, but it didn't register until the black pickup pulled into Mac's, drove past the blacksmith shop, and straight across the lawn toward Mac on his rocker on the porch.

The truck was going so fast I thought it was going to plough into everything—Mac, the porch and rockers, and the house.

Then the truck suddenly braked. A big man jumped out of the cab and grabbed Mac as he reached for his .22, which was leaning against the wall behind him. He threw Mac to the ground. I let out a screech but they couldn't hear me from the bottom of the hill. Two other men got out of the cab. One of them was wearing an army uniform, and he pointed a rifle at Mac. The other two propped Mac up against one of the porch pillars and they all seemed to be yelling at him.

The big man was pointing up to the graveyard. They were pointing right at me but there was no way they could see me on my knees behind the oats and sumac.

I turned and ran low over to the church, but the door was locked. I ran toward the back of the priest's house and saw Marian's little girl in the backyard. I jumped up the stairs and shouted through the screen door at Marian, who was standing in the back kitchen.

"They're killing Mac! They're going to shoot him!" I shouted.

She came right out without asking questions and said, "Show me."

I guided her around the back of the church over to where I knew we could look down without being seen.

There was Mac sitting on the ground in the hot sun without his hat, and now two of them had guns pointed at him.

Marian said, "You stay here and watch them. I have to use the telephone. I'll be right back."

She ran to her back door and dragged little Lise inside. About a minute later, the screen door slammed, and she came running but stopped at the back door of the church.

She had a ring of keys. She opened the door to the sacristy and disappeared inside. I kept watching the men around Mac.

The big one was pacing back and forth and looked like he was screaming at Mac.

Suddenly the church bell rang. There was a pause, and then it rang again. And then again and again. Four slow tolls. It seemed forever as I watched the three men turn and look up toward the church steeple. I turned and ran to the back of the church just as Marian came out. She locked the sacristy and we both ran to the house, and Marian ran around locking doors and closing curtains. Then we peeked through the curtains where we could see the front corner of the church and across to the graveyard.

"Why did you ring the bells?" I asked.

She hesitated.

"Well, for one thing it should make those clods think twice about what they're up to."

"But they'll come up here, now."

"I hope they do, and leave Mac alone. They don't really want us." Then she said, "So I'm going out there. You stay and watch Lise." And with that she grabbed the ring of keys and ran out the back door and into the lane just as the black truck came swerving up to the front of the church.

Marian walked toward the truck swinging her key chain as if she was out for a stroll. I put Lise in her crib and ran out the door behind Marian.

By now the big man was pulling on the locked church door. He wore a red glove on the hand that he wasn't using.

"Can I help you?" Marian shouted.

"Who's ringing the goddamned bell?"

"I did," Marian answered calmly. "I don't know why it's any of your business, but I just got the call to ring the toll for old man Doyle. It's his death knell. Those are my instructions from Father Foley. Why? Did I wake you from your nap?"

The big man looked confused. "Stupid fuckin' dogans. Doyle died two days ago." Then he squinted, and said, "Don't I know you, lady?"

Marian said, "No, but I know you, Munro."

Munro started toward Marian, but the army man who was kneeling in the back of the truck barked, "We're on our way to check out your graveyard, and then we'll be wanting to talk to your priest." Then he banged on the roof of the truck and shouted, "Back up across the road and into the graveyard."

Munro followed the truck and turned to leer at Marian.

"I'll be back," he said. She just laughed at him.

We watched as they backed up the centre path of the cemetery and stopped, and then two of them hauled Mac out of the back of the truck. They started to walk toward the grave that had just been dug for Doyle. They had to help Mac walk.

"Hey, what are you doing there with Old Mac?" Marian shouted.

"Shut your gob and go home, lady. This is official government business. I'm a corporal in His Majesty's Army," the army man shouted back.

Suddenly the two others threw Mac into Doyle's empty hole. Mac had been claustrophobic since his fall in the well. He'd have a heart attack.

Marian started striding forward with her fists clenched. I followed her and when I looked to my right I saw a flatbed coming south with a few men standing in the back of the truck. They looked like they could be going to the Low parade. They pulled up behind me alongside the cemetery, jumped out of the truck, and just stood there like zombies, like they were waiting on something.

The army guy and the two others turned and stared at them. I recognized Barry O.

Then I heard a truck coming up the hill from the south. Three men jumped out of the back and stood there just like the first bunch of zombies as Père Beaubien got out of the passenger seat. He strutted up and into the graveyard with his hand on his cross and his big beads swaying against his cassock.

Marian ran over to Père and said something.

151

"Vandals? What are you doing in our graveyard? You're defiling our sacred ground."

Mac was nowhere to be seen below the level of the grave so I ran over while the yelling was going on. He was down there in the hole looking poorly.

"Don't tell them anything we know about the zombie grave, Raymond," Mac gasped.

Munro suddenly went crazy for some reason. He pointed at Beaubien and shouted, "You, you son of a bitch. You phony black bastard. You see this hand?" He swung the hand and wrist like a club and it landed near Beaubien's neck and I could hear a crack.

Grafftey was shouting, "No, Munro, it's not —"

But it was too late. Munro was raging, "You fuckin' dogan bastard!" and with his rifle raised in the claw and his other hand he was about to slam the butt into Beaubien's head as he lay unconscious on the ground.

Everything that happened after that was almost invisible, it happened so fast. There was a godawful howl. Suddenly a foot and leg flew through the air and Munro's head seemed to snap from his shoulders. There were some whirling black boots. They flew, hit the other man and sent him backwards over a gravestone.

I was staring at the back of a cop uniform that picked up the army guy and slammed him against his own truck. His head hit with a crack and he slid to the ground. The cop then knelt down beside Mac's grave, and others came and lifted Mac out of the hole. The cop picked up Mac like he was a baby and carried him back through the watching men who parted and then closed after he passed.

I ran to get a better look. This had to be ZombieMan. As I looked to see what he was doing with Mac, ZombieMan turned his head a little and shouted back at Marian, "Take care of Père."

Marian did a cute little curtsey toward ZombieMan and then turned and with a few others circled Père Beaubien, who was still lying on the ground.

Marian knelt beside Beaubien. "I think his collarbone is broken," she said. "We'll have to get him to Dr. Barbee in Wakefield."

The truck that had come from the north did a U-turn in front of the church and headed back up the road with Mac in it. Beaubien was put in the truck he came in, which did a U-turn and headed south. Mad Munro and his friend and the army man hadn't moved a muscle.

Marian led me back across the road to the house, where we sat on the front porch just watching the remaining men stare at the three bodies lying around the army truck. Soon I heard a faint siren coming up the river from way down below.

I always wondered why the cops gave crooks so much warning. When the others heard the siren, they waved at Marian and started disappearing up and down the road, leaving the three men just lying there in the graveyard.

I told the police that I never clearly saw the whirling howling man, and that was true. I didn't mention the uniform, but it looked just like the one the policemen were wearing. Marian said the same thing, and said she'd never seen him before, but I knew that wasn't true. The QPP didn't seem to care one way or the other, and soon they were joined by two more policemen in another car and they all spent their time tending to a man lying in the graveyard unconscious, and talking to the army man who was sitting with his legs spread and his head resting back against one of the big truck tires. It was getting dark but I didn't see the big guy.

Finally, they all drove away with one of the policemen driving the army truck. There was no one left in the graveyard.

I sat there for a few minutes talking to Marian.

"Why did all those people show up, Miss Marian?"

"Well, Ma Bell and church bells can do wonders, Raymond. Now, would you like something to eat? Lise will be wanting her dinner."

But I didn't want anything to eat. I suddenly felt very tired, and I had terrible cramps, and needed to go to the bathroom to do number two, but I wasn't going to say all that to pretty Marian.

"No, I want to go back down the hill."

"But I don't think Mac will be back tonight, Raymond. You should sleep here."

"No, I'll go in to Cals'. They expect me anyway." And I rushed down the hill.

When I got down the hill, it was getting dark. I picked up Mac's gun, which was still lying there by the porch, and then went into the outhouse. I was so full of fart, I had to have a sit.

In all the books I'd ever read, even *Nicholas Nickleby*, they never talked about having to go to the bathroom. I fell asleep on my throne thinking about that.

I woke up to strange noises. What I saw through the cracks of the outhouse was the black weathered wood of the shop dissolving into the sky. Then I felt the heat. It was such a forceful fire that my face still feels it today when I stare at fire. It's like my face has its own memory.

I pulled up my pants, but as I pushed the door open I saw a man's back. He was pouring something while shuffling toward Mac's farmhouse. Everything was illuminated by the blaze. I could see the man was using Mac's gasoline can, and the hand holding the can was red.

"No, please, God. Not Mac's house," I moaned.

I closed the door and grabbed Mac's gun. It was hot. I was filled with fear. I could hear the cinders hitting the wall of the outhouse and the roar from the shop, and my back was scorching.

I felt like I was going to explode in there. I was going to die.

I remembered what Mac said. "You only need one shot if

you get it right."

I pushed the door open with my bum, raised the gun and shot at the big bent-over target only ten yards away. I pretended it was a pea soup can and hit Red Hand right in the arse. He dropped the can to grab his arse, and the can exploded when it hit the ground, and Red Hand screamed his guts out.

I ran like crazy, with the fire blazing behind me. I ran past the house and toward the back gully. I could still hear Hand. It was a long, strange shriek now.

I was scared like crazy but I threw Mac's gun behind the chicken coop as I passed so I'd know where it was.

I raced through the field of oats toward the back barn, and then I heard horns blowing and saw a truck racing up the hill. The volunteer firemen would soon be coming in Cal Road as well, so I stuck to the field and ran even harder. I didn't want to see anyone.

On the ridge behind the back barn, I stumbled, then stood up to look behind me.

The shop was soaring into the sky. The whole shebang gone up in flames. The clouds were cluttered with smoke that was blocking most of the moon, but I could see that the house was still not burning. There was no sign of Red Hand.

I continued toward Cals' through the bush and across the fields and heard more trucks racing by on Cal Road. When I got to the house, the lights were on, but no one was around. Martin and Mabel were probably at the fire.

I crept up the back stairs, and there was Billy lying on the landing out cold. I leaned forward to see if he was dead or something, and then I could smell the booze. I stepped over Billy and went up to peek in Martin and Mabel's bedroom, but they weren't there. I went down the few steps to the landing and started pulling at Billy to get up and come to bed. He moaned and shoved at me but soon I had him crawling up the stairs and he collapsed into the room. I kicked his legs out of the way and shut the door.

Brian was in bed watching and laughing.

"Where in hell did you find him? Wherever it was, you shoulda left him."

I took off half my clothes and lay down beside Brian. He was almost asleep again. He sure could laugh and sleep.

I heard sirens.

"What's going on out there?" Brian mumbled.

"I don't know."

Brian fell asleep quickly. I lay there and listened to the sirens, and trembled, and took a long time to fall asleep.

EIGHTEEN

August 1947

MAC AWOKE TO the smell of coffee, the sounds of birds, and the sight of leaves brushing sky, which he could see through the smoke hole at the top of the teepee. He had woken during the night to gaze at clusters of stars.

He heard murmuring voices and could smell a campfire but, looking over at the small pit at the centre of the teepee, the night fire had burnt out. Three sleeping bags were rolled up and tucked against the wall of the tent.

Mac lay back and closed his eyes. He felt totally tranquil and wanted to freeze the feeling.

He recalled the previous evening. It had ended at the outdoor fire pit over a meal of bean stew with bread and long conversation.

"It seems that you, too, have been given victory o'er the grave, Mac," Mondou had said at one point. Later he offered Mac a shot of fine rye whiskey for medicinal purposes. "I'm afraid Murph will leave home if I don't show such hospitality, Old Mac." Murph was pulling out the tin cups before Mac could respond.

"It's the best mash in the country," he boasted.

Mac agreed to a wee dram. He drank huddled in a sleeping bag by the fire, still feeling sore in his shoulders and lower back.

He had a second dram and thought he could feel himself healing. He even vaguely remembered singing,

Just a simple little ditty,
In her good ould Irish way,
And I'd give the world if she could sing
That song to me this day.
Too-ra-loo-ra-loo-ra, too-ra-loo-ra-li.

He then vaguely remembered being dragged in his sleeping bag into the tent. He smiled to himself with eyes still closed, thinking, *Is this the Hereafter?*

Now Mondou crawled into the tent and sat cross-legged and stared at Mac.

Mac opened one eye and said, "Living well is the best revenge, Mondou." Then he raised himself on one elbow. "Did someone deliver my note to Raymond at Cals'?"

"Yes, Mac. Raymond was in bed. Billy will see that he reads it."

Billy . . . one of the band?

Mac sat up and tried to sit like Mondou, but then settled for resting his back on the tent pole.

"I have much news, Mac. Some of it bad. Some of it, with God's forgiveness, very good."

Mac nodded and Mondou continued.

"Somehow Munro slipped away from the graveyard before the QPP could take him away. He waited until nightfall and then burned down your blacksmith shop. Your house is fine, but Munro exploded into a tongue of flame on your front lawn. He's dead."

"What's the bad news?"

Mondou laughed. "All the rest is good news. I suppose your blacksmith shop is a . . . loss."

"Ah, poor Rita. Her antique shop is now a crypt. Never do now what you can put off to another day, Mondou. It would have taken me years to arrange that place to her satisfaction." Mac sat and cackled, while Mondou stood and stuck his head outside the tent. He turned back to Mac.

"Can you handle more good news, Mac?" Mondou pulled the flaps of the tent back further and said, "Ox has sought redemption."

Mac looked out. Ox was standing in front of the tent, and he wasn't alone.

Mac stared. His mouth hung slack as he looked into the eyes of the big Algonquin.

"For the boy," Ox said.

NINETEEN

August 1947

I'D JUST PICKED up the last two pails of milk when Aunt Mabel came stomping her big rubber boots into the barn like she was knee-deep in manure. You couldn't carry just one pail of milk because you'd have no balance and slop too much milk on the way to the dairy, and then catch hell about spilling what cow and man spent half a day producing.

"Raymond, what are you doin' up here?" she said. "I thought I told you to go back to bed this morning. Put those pails down and come with me. Your mom's down at the house. You must be dead tired. Up half the night, and after all you bin through. But don't sleep with Brian anymore. We just found out he's got the TB."

We were rounding the corner of the dairy now, and I could see Mom and Gertie standing on the lawn on the far side of the house.

My mother was coming at me as fast as I'd ever seen her move, and staring me up and down. Then we hugged.

"Are you okay, Raymond?"

I nodded, and Aunt Mabel said, "He's fine, Rita. I'll get us some tea."

Soon we had taken off our boots in the mud room, and Mom and I sat at the kitchen table while Aunt Mabel buzzed around getting tea.

"Well, Raymond," she called out, "there's a lot to tell, so you'd better get started. Your boy's had quite a week, Rita."

I started to tumble it out. "Mom, Smoky is dead. He was killed by zombies, but not the movie kind. The war zombies did it."

Aunt Gertie groaned, "Oh, dear me," as Mom ran around the table and knelt and hugged me.

"Oh, Raymond, Raymond. Not Smoky. Why would anyone want to kill Smoky?" I could see Aunt Mabel over my mom's shoulder spinning her finger like she wanted me to keep talking. She clearly wasn't going to say much, probably because she didn't know half of it anyway.

I kept going.

"Mom, when you get in to Mac's you'll see that the shop is burned down, and most of the grass in front of the house because they were trying to burn it down, too."

Mom had framed my head in her hands by now and was looking at me like she thought I was crazy.

"Where's Mac?" she said.

"He was kidnapped by the zombies." I thought my mom might faint now as she sat back on her haunches and looked over at Aunt Mabel, who had just sat beside her with the tea.

"Here, Rita. This note is from Mac and it was on our kitchen table this morning. We heard the dogs howlin' in the night but thought it was the coyotes got 'em fussed. It's addressed to you and Raymond, but Martin read it before he went up for the milkin' and said Old Mac's fine."

Mom flipped open the note, read it, and said, "He wants you to know he's with the good zombies, Raymond. He says it's nice to be on the inside looking out, and he won't be home until he's sure the crazies are put away." Then Mom smiled. "He says maybe we'll do the sleigh ride at Christmas. It's him, all right. He also says 'I love you, Raymond. You're invincible,' and then there's this funny symbol on the bottom."

I grabbed the note. It was the zombie sign, the ChiZRho,

161

with the Z and not the X.

Mom just kept shaking her head from side to side.

"How can they be good zombies if they kill dogs and burn down farmhouses?"

"Mom, it wasn't the zombies who tried to burn down the farmhouse. It was a guy with a red hand but I shot him in the arse. Then he dropped the gas can and burned himself, and screamed like a madman. I think I killed him but I didn't mean to so it's a venial sin."

Now my mom had her own head in her hands and said through her fingers, "Raymond, I've only been gone a week. Lord God Almighty, how could all this happen in a week? Tell me it's all a joke."

Aunt Mabel put her arm around my mom, who was still kneeling on the floor in front of me.

I was thinking I should give Mom a rest. It was a lot to swallow all at once. "Where did you get the gun?" she finally whispered.

"I used Mac's gun. It was lying by the house where he dropped it when the Red Hand band took Mac up to the cemetery yesterday to bury him alive."

Mom started to choke. I had started back into the story too quickly. I thought I'd slip in an easy one.

"I think the outhouse was burning down too when I was running away but I didn't want to look back and see Red Hand burning up so I'm not sure."

Now I could see that even Aunt Mabel was looking at me strange, but she said, "The outhouse is gone, Rita, but Mac's place is fine. They watered it down and the wind kept blowing to the east and it wasn't touched."

I was so happy to hear that, I almost cried.

Mom had another long blink, and then sighed a long sigh, and then took my face in her hands again.

"Oh, Raymond, after all you've been through, how can you be okay?"

"Because I'm invincible, Mom. Incapable of being vanquished. Unbeatable . . ." And I proudly went through my definition.

I knew Mom wanted to get me back to Ottawa, but there was much to do before we left. We walked around the black carcass of the antique shop. Some of it was still smouldering. I thought Mom was going to cry. Aunt Gertie was supposed to be helping us clean up the mess but she was busy working the phone and party lines to learn all she could about the events of the past day.

I told Mom a few times that I had to say a real goodbye to Smoky before we left because we might not be back until Thanksgiving. I hated the word "goodbye" now because good-bye was forever. Even though I had killed a man, saying goodbye to Smoky felt worse.

Mom said she wanted to come up to Smoky's grave with me, but first she had to get Gertie off the phone and get some cleaning and closing done. Mac might not be home for a while.

I helped Mom and then got away when Aunt Gertie was back on the job. I wanted to find Mac's .22 and put it in a safe place before I went home.

It was about where I thought it would be, lying way down in the oats behind the coop. Although it was just a one-shot, I made sure it was empty, just like Mac always did, and then snuck into the farmhouse and placed it behind Mac's books under his cot where he kept it at night.

Mom called me for lunch, but I couldn't move. She left me alone staring up the hill. Later, she came out and put her hand on my shoulder.

"We'll go up as soon as you have a sandwich," she said. I didn't want to eat but I went with her. The phone rang just as Mom and I went into the house.

Mom grabbed the phone before Aunt Gertie could get up and reach it. She shook her head no, it wasn't for Gertie. She just seemed to listen mostly. She said okay and then hung up.

"Who was that?"

"Nothing important, Gertie. I'm thinking, Raymond, that maybe it's best that we visit Smoky now while Gertie wraps up your sandwich and packs up. You can eat in the car on the way to town if you feel like it."

Mom and I walked around the burned shop and started up the hill.

"It will never be the same in Ottawa, either, without Smoky," I said. "We have to get rid of his red box in the basement. Who will run down the cut with me? Roll in the leaves at LeBreton with me?" At first I was gagging but now my talk was speeding up like I couldn't control it. "Smoky chases toward me every day when I hit the bridge coming from school, Mom."

I started to blubber and stopped walking. Mom just stopped with me and put her hand on my shoulder.

"You know what I said to Mac, Mom? 'Cross my heart, I hope to die and be buried beside Smoky.'"

Mom started to cry. I had to fix myself somehow. I was not being invincible.

We reached the graveyard and I ran around and knelt at the fence and looked down at the stone and the fresh digging, and I tried to pray. Mom came up behind me, and stood with her rosary.

It was a waste of time trying to pray. I kept thinking about how many things wouldn't be the same, and the list went on forever.

I'd have to explain to all my friends in Ottawa because Smoky was not only my dog—he was the Plymouth Street dog. He was the only dog who would follow us everywhere, even on our bikes. Up to Lansdowne, down to Dow's Lake, over to the Experimental Farm . . . Smoky would come along if we didn't lock him up.

I said a quick Our Father, Hail Mary and Glory Be and got up, knowing Mom must want to leave. I looked up at her and said again through tears, "It will never be the same." I was shaking.

She had a weird sort of look and said, "Marian wants to say goodbye to you," and she craned her neck and looked over toward the church.

Mom held my shoulders as we started walking toward the front of the cemetery.

"Here they come," Mom waved.

I looked across the road and Marian was running toward us waving her hands in that goofy way, and her little girl was trying to do the same.

And bounding along beside them was a dog. He was black, with a white throat, and he wore a red bandana.

Epilogue

Remember, Raymond?
Remember that?
How could you forget?

I'd been grazing through Mac's ledger for hours. I stretched back from the table, squeezing complaints out of Mac's old chair, and stared through the window out into the twilight. I could see the final fire of the setting sun on the pines up behind the graveyard.

I went out to the porch, reached into the cooler, pulled an iced bottle from its nest, twisted off the cap and put it in my pocket—controlling trash and keeping count, I liked to say. I leaned against the pillar and looked up at the church and Smoky's grave.

Had the hill not been much higher back then?

Smoky Two was never quite like the original Smoky. It wasn't his fault. Neither Mac nor I had the patience to teach him all the tricks. But I loved him, too. He lived until he was fourteen or so, and just died of old age. Not like Smoky.

I'd be planting Smoky Two's ashes beside Smoky's grave in the morning. Better late than never.

I knew so little back then. My mother had hustled me back

to Ottawa, worried about Brian's TB diagnosis, about whether I was traumatized by the shooting of Munro. But the days after that were so busy, what with shopping and doctor's appointments and showing Smoky his new home, introducing him to my friends and rolling in the leaves at LeBreton. I was back at school, of course, and riding my bike to the movies. Even a zombie movie or two, I recall.

I lit the lamps, put a can of Habitant into a pot to simmer and returned to the contents of Mac's ledger, which lay scattered across the dining-room table. Newspaper clippings, maps of the Laurentians along with others drawn by Mac, a bumper sticker for the Longest Bar in the Gatineau, which Mac never got around to putting on his jalopy. It was clipped to an article that said the bar had burned down, and Mac had scrawled "Popeye" across it. There were photos of Gertie and Mom, and of Mac and me standing in front of his jalopy, letters from an Ottawa archivist, much about other crimes that seemed to concern Mac, and again, the worn, soiled, brown leather book with one printed word on the inside page: Ephemeris. I still couldn't make heads or tails of it because it was written in both English and Latin, and was not Mac's handwriting. The tone of the writing led me to suspect it was written by a priest. I set it aside again. I had already found out so much about our week in 1947 that I was surprised I hadn't found the answer to my one big question.

Who was buried in Mondou's grave?

His good priest had provided a cadaver to place in a grave. That may have been enough for Mondou. It would not have been enough for my old Mac.

And suddenly, there it was in front of me. Like a zombie, Mac had come back.

It was an envelope labelled, "For Your Eyes Only. You're old enough to keep this secret now."

Since I was sixty years old, Mac was guilty of understatement. Or was he?

Dear Raymond,

I loved puzzles, and Proulx puzzled me, as you probably remember. Often he seemed bull-dumb, and he could be dangerous, yet he was so radically devout. If you give that a little thought, it's a terrifying triangle. The old fool almost killed me once with that peavey he always carried when I cursed his beloved Père for abandoning the poor dead souls across in the grove.

You know me, Raymond. Holding in a good barb was like sitting on a fart. I knew that Proulx had hidden an American draft dodger in his barn, but I never got out of him who he was or where he went. Proulx just said the name was Sam, and that he paid handsomely for the privilege of living in his barn. But I kept asking him about it every time he visited, just to get his goat.

Then one night, after years of being badgered, he blurts it out: "Found him floating on the marsh side of McGoey Dam without his head."

And that, Raymond, was the sound of Proulx's spigot turning on. By the time I was finished with him, he had talked and cried and talked and cried and confessed that he had confessed his very mortal sin to Beaubien years earlier so he had nothing to worry about.

Turned out that one night when his tenant was out, Proulx went into the barn for a snoop. Underneath a sleeping bag he found something that looked like a big radio with wires coming out that were hooked up to the rafters.

The American was a German spy, Raymond. His real name was Siegfried! It took me a long while to figure it all out, but that's another story.

So old Proulx is standing there in his barn trying to put it together in his not-too-quick way, when in walks Sam, and he's holding a gun, like a little gangster gun from the movies. He's pointing it at Proulx and looking like he'll do evil.

"I put my hand on my heart, Mac," Proulx says, "like I do when you blaspheme, and bent over like I was going to fall down with an attack, but instead I lifted my peavey and slashed at him. His head was half off after I swung a few more times. He was bleeding in the hay like a butchered pig. I couldn't stop the blood so I rolled in the manure wagon, loaded him in and dumped him off the dam into the marsh to let him bleed off."

So Proulx goes back to the barn and spreads hay around to soak up the blood and loads it into the wagon and goes back to the marsh to dump it in the same place and wouldn't ya know the head is sticking up. Proulx figures it's because it's only half off so he walks out on a dead tree, hauls the whole thing in with his scythe and takes the head clean off, pushes the body back in the marsh, puts the head in a flour bag and buries it deep in the sawdust in his ice shed.

In his ice shed!

I would never tell Proulx he was smart because that would be a lie, but he was not the right man to try and hide a cadaver, that's for sure. He goes back the next morning and looks down from the dam and he can still see the body. It won't sink!

So he runs the manure cart back down to the dam, pulls the body out of the marsh and buries it beside the head at the bottom of the ice shed. And then runs to the confessional to confess his sins to Père Beaubien.

I call the whole thing the case of the convenient corpse, because as you well know, Père had a very good use for that body.

So in the end we have a headless German spy buried in St. Martin's graveyard. He's had a Catholic funeral and was sprinkled with holy water by Père, who begged angels to lead him into paradise.

Burying Smoky in the sanctified graveyard would have been less scandalous, don't you think?

As for Mondou, maybe he knew more about his own corpse than he admitted, but I think he did not. Père Beaubien would not risk everlasting hellfire by betraying his confessional oath. I suppose it didn't matter much. No one could have restored a life lost to Proulx's peavey.

I know what you're thinking, Raymond. What about the damned head? Well, years later, Proulx brought in the electricity, bought a refrigerator, and wanted to tear down the ice shed but didn't think Marie would like a spy's head in her brand-new Frigidaire.

But by now he's spooked by the head and doesn't want to move it again. So who does he come to for help?

I thought about it a lot, Raymond. Just say no to Proulx. Call the cops, who would open graves, make charges, seek out ZombieMan, arrest Père Beaubien, who was by that time in the order's retirement home in Ayersville, find Father Foley at his new parish in Arnprior and then involve me and you . . .

Where would the ball of string end?

So, late one night Proulx and I dug up the head, which was still frozen. We dumped it in another flour bag, and I put it on the jalopy's rumble seat while Proulx stood there crossing himself and mumbling French prayers and talking about *feux follets*. I rushed the head up to the back of the cemetery and buried it in a hole I'd dug in the grove along the cemetery fence, only fifty yards from the rest of the body.

And there it lies still. If you're curious enough to take a look, I've marked it so you'll know.

Just one more secret buried in Martindale.

So much for truth, eh, Raymond?

Beyond the Proulx murder there was much information buried in Mac's ledger related to the people and the events of that week in August 1947.

The Canadian government eventually pardoned most zombies, but Mondou was never pardoned, nor was he ever caught. Marian and little Lise left Martindale before long. Rumour had it she and Mondou lived out their days in the Laurentians and that their six children were still running *le syndicat*.

Grafftey was given two choices. Retire from the army or accept another demotion with a transfer to Terrace, British Columbia. He chose to retire and later became a commission-aire at the Parliament Buildings in Ottawa.

After Munro burned himself to death, Popeye spent time in the Bordeaux Penitentiary in Montreal for firebombing "The Longest Bar in the Gatineau."

Ox and Murph both died too young of natural causes but, as Mac wrote, "You could not call their gallivanting natural."

And Mac? He continued to snoop while annoying everyone in the process until his death in 1971.

I shuffled all the papers back into their piles and pushed them and the ledger to one side. I'd take a closer look at them another day. Perhaps I'd do some scribbling and deep thinking and nosing around of my own.

Maybe even write a book.

That'd please Old Mac.

NOT EXACTLY THE END

I knew of several barns where I thought the past might lie.
— E.B. White

Author's Note

WHILE I WAS WRITING this tale about Canada's zombies, there was an on-going probe for truth in Canada concerning Afghan prisoner abuse. Politicians, rights groups, journalists, diplomats, and interested citizens were using an arsenal of modern technology, updated disclosure laws, and hearings to determine whether Canada's handling of a limited number of prisoners broke domestic or international law. It would seem a simple search through recent history, but the system has not revealed its truth as yet.

Contrast the Afghan probe with the statement of World War II historian Daniel Byers that "nothing much can be proven about the mistreatment of zombies during World War II." There's a good reason. Byers's doctoral thesis is still the only considerable history written on the issue of the National Resources Mobilization Act and zombies.

After almost seventy years, the absolute minimum has been written about the zombies, compared to tens of millions of words written about an estimated 163 Afghan detainees. Just as critical, however, is the difference in approach.

Unlike the Afghan probe, politicians, the Canadian military, a co-operative wartime press, bureaucrats, and zombie tormentors all ensured that there was little recorded about the zombies under the guise of protecting the war effort. During the war, Germans read more about Canada's zombies and Canada's military mutinies than was read by the average Canadian. And although the Canadian government apologized to many groups over the years, it never offered an apology to the 157,841 citizen zombies of World War II, whether they went Active or not.

Only decades later, Daniel Byers admitted that "the evidence does exist that it [abuse] occurred," but if we cannot uncover the truth about Afghan detainees in current time, I fear the truth of seventy years ago will die out with the last remaining zombie.

ABOUT THE AUTHOR

Not Exactly a War Hero is Ray's first book.

After years as the CEO of a multinational, he wanted to try something entrepreneurial that required nothing more than paper, pencils, and time.

Ray has been summering in the Gatineau Hills for his whole remembered life.

TO ORDER MORE COPIES:

GENERAL STORE PUBLISHING HOUSE INC.

499 O'Brien Rd., Renfrew, Ontario, Canada K7V 3Z3
Tel. 1.800.465.6072 • Fax 1.613.432.3634
www.gsph.com